SOUTH 1982

About the author

Adrián N. Bravi was born in San Fernando, Buenos Aires in 1963, and lives in Italy, where he works as a librarian. *Sud 1982* was published in 2008. Other novels include *La pelusa* (2007, English translation, *Dust*, 2017), *Il riporto* (2010, English translation, *The Combover*, 2013), *L'albero e la vacca* (2013), *L'inondazione* (2015), *La gelosia delle lingue* (2017), *L'idioma di Casilda Moreira* (2019) and *Il levitatore* (2020).

About the translator

Richard Dixon lives and works in Italy. His translation of Adrián N. Bravi's novel *The Combover* was published in 2013. Other translations include the last works of Umberto Eco (*The Prague Cemetery, Numero Zero,* and several collections of essays), Roberto Calasso (*Ardor, The Art of the Publisher, The Ruin of Kasch, The Unnamable Present, The Celestial Hunter*), Giacomo Leopardi (*Zibaldone,* as co-translator), Carlo Emilio Gadda (*The Experience of Pain*), Paolo Volponi (*The Javelin Thrower*), Antonio Moresco (*Distant Light, Clandestinity*), Stefano Massini (*The Lehman Trilogy, The Book of Nonexistent Words*) and Marcello Fois (*Valse Triste*).

Adrián N. Bravi

SOUTH 1982

Translated from the Italian by Richard Dixon

London
*Jet*stone
2022

A *Jet*stone paperback.

ISBN 9781910858233

Originally published in Italian in 2008
by nottetempo as *Sud 1982*.

The cover shows a detail from "British sailors from HMS Cardiff ashore
Pebble Island, June 1982" by Ken Griffiths, reproduced under the Creative
Commons Attribution-Share Alike 4.0 International licence (from
https://commons.wikimedia.org/wiki/File:Falklands_1982.jpg).

Cover design by The Ever-Shifting Subject.

"In order to forget the past," said Irlandés,
"you first need a monument to remember it."

Chapter One

In which I leave the barracks behind me and get headaches that pain me at night, when the world starts turning the wrong way round

Fernando Huidobro and I were staring silently at the barracks corridor and the flights of stairs we had cleaned hundreds of times. Each of us was carrying a green kitbag of clothes around our necks and our uniforms hanging from a wire coat-hanger. We had been standing in front of the NCO office for two hours, waiting for our clothing to be handed back. The idea of being discharged, however imminent, seemed remoter than ever. There was always a painful ration of waiting for everything, whatever it was. In cases like ours there were no specific rules and we had to hope some stressed-out NCO would tire of seeing us each time he went in and out of the office. All we could do then was wait patiently for the last formalities to be sorted out. And Huidobro, being a good soldier, stood looking down the corridor, the far end of which was echoing with the voices of soldiers on their return from duty.

"We can wander round the city centre if you like, as soon as we're out," I suggested, just for something to say, but Huidobro made no reply and carried on staring down the corridor, not looking back. "Or we could have a coffee at the station."

I hadn't heard him speak for a while and didn't expect him to do so then. I just wanted to figure out what I would do once the barrier had gone up at the entrance gate. Would I close myself up in a cinema or a bar, or take a walk round the Palermo gardens? I wasn't used to the idea of one night being followed by a tomorrow. *You don't have to think about anything, soldier. Just obey your orders.*

And if I tell you there's no tomorrow, then you'd better be sure to get it all done today.

Over the next few days, once I had left the barracks, I was ready to face whatever happened, though I expected nothing in particular, as if I were living in a time all to be filled up; but, since nothing ever happened apart from the usual things and I had no idea how to occupy those long days, I used to set off each day following a straight line that started around ten in the morning and ended around three at night, when I returned home through the pitch darkness of the city. The streets were beautiful at that hour, empty of the chaos of the daytime world, and I walked along that maze of roads that joined up here and there and kept me walking through the night. I wandered about and my mind at that hour was full of thoughts and memories I couldn't get out of my head. I thought a lot about the things that had happened, things I wanted to unload and then, hopefully, to carry on walking without a care, without being weighed down by those thoughts. I wanted my brain to be like the night, a great emptiness that was dark inside, and then to fill it up with one or two beers, three at most, and return home through that maze of streets. Life at that hour seemed worth living, unlike the day; but then, when I arrived home and looked at the lock on the door, and that boundless space shrank down to a sort of moving hole that swayed from right to left as I tried to push the key into it, the world went back to what it was.

I was nineteen then, just back from the Malvinas. I slept badly and used to wake at night dripping with sweat. I had few friends, and, like so many of my age who aimed for the sublime, I suffered from headaches. The pain wasn't that strong, even if more than once I had to cover every window and rest, not eating, with a wet cloth over my forehead. They were pains you could hardly feel but were enough to take up the whole of my day. I generally got them in the morning, over my right eye, while those I got in the evening pounded away over my left eye. This alternation was strange, as our next-door neighbour also agreed, though his pains were at the back of his head; but unlike me he thought it was all right that things were the way they were, whereas for me, being one who aimed for the sublime, it all seemed like a filthy trick. As time went by, my headaches had converted me into an unbeliever. I was convinced, on thinking about it, that if God existed then headaches could not; and so, if my headache existed, it seemed obvious there was no God.

I was about to reach a crucial moment in my life, I'd been expecting it for some time: I either sorted myself out and started working, or I would start again from scratch, go off and live somewhere else; neither option ruled out the fact that either way I'd have to earn a living. I had thought a lot about it before finding an answer to the problem. These days were crucial. I was putting my whole life, my body and soul, at risk. It wasn't something to sort out just like that. If I had turned left, for example, I couldn't have gone right, and if I'd turned right then I couldn't have gone left. So it was better to wait and push straight ahead. And that was what I'd been doing for quite some time once I'd left the army: I left home early, wandered around the local streets, went to the library to read Plotinus and in the evening closed myself up drinking beer at Tío Pablo's. It seemed the most reasonable way of dealing with those confused, interminable days of long sun-filled afternoons. Those days, for me, represented such an immensity of time that just the thought of having to wait for the evening made me ill. Then I imagined that one day, coming home, I'd be sucked into a great vortex and hurled off to some distant place, where I would have woken up and gotten over all the effects of war. But each time I hit against the same, identical story. I used to come home at night from Tío Pablo's, crossing the dark city, would stop each time to empty my bladder against the wall of some house while I sang *Yo tenía un amor, un amor muy bello*, would shake away the last lingering drops

9

and then continue walking. When I arrived home, I'd pause for a while in front of the door, try to find the keyhole, utter two or three curses, then give the door a good kick. I used to tell myself: "Enough, fuck it! I've got to stop! Not another drop!" My mother would hear me swearing and would get out of bed. Then she'd start repeating that I shouldn't be going to Tío Pablo's every evening, that it was no place for me, that I'd learn nothing from those no-good drunkards, that it was time to start studying, to go to university and so on. I'm sure she'd have liked to see me with a university degree rolled up under my arm, like many of my old school friends who had already worked out their futures by the age of fourteen, but for me it was already a miracle I had got through school in one piece, considering how many evenings I used to spend at Tío Pablo's. At that point I'd go berserk and tell my mother this house was no place for me either. And yet I always went back, despite everything. And with no more ado I'd lock myself in my room.

"Everyone has a right to do what the fuck he likes," I used to mutter.

My head whirled in all directions. I took an aspirin and ducked under the sheets. I started to breathe slowly. I breathed in with my chest, out with my stomach, in with my chest, out with my stomach, until the flow of air swept my thoughts away and I fell asleep. At that, the world would start turning the right way round, but after three or four hours of sleep it would change direction and I would wake up trying to take cover behind an armoured tank from a hail of bullets. "Don't shoot, don't shoot," I'd yell. I would get out of bed, straighten the sheets, take a gulp of cold water to get the nightmare off my mind. If I was lucky, I'd go back to sleep until the next blast of gunfire; otherwise, this would mark the beginning of my day.

*

So here we are then, on that July day in the barracks, ready to hand back our clothing and leave that place behind us. We weren't bothered about having to wait two hours standing in front of the NCO office, by the staircase that stank of bleach. We weren't in any hurry to get away, even though each of us would soon be trying as hard as we could to forget all about this place. We had often found ourselves alone, Fernando Huidobro and me, thinking about what we would do once we got back home, once we'd got away from those islands. But now we had to sort ourselves out; and sorting ourselves out, during that winter month of 1982, served no purpose for the future – it served simply to smooth over the past and to accept it for what it was. Go into tomorrow backward, my father used to say.

Meanwhile, two recruits had come down the steps wearing green combat trousers and boots two sizes too large. They were carrying the leftovers of their mess rations to the kitchen and were leaving black greasy footprints on the stairs with each step. If it had been a day like any other, Huidobro and I would have ended up at the top of the first landing washing away those footprints from top to bottom. Luckily, we were already halfway out of there and couldn't care a damn about those prints on the stairs.

From the window we could see two recruits gathering fallen leaves from the plane trees, their shaved heads puckered by the cold. One prodded the leaves with a sharp spike, putting them into a hemp sack, while the other made small piles with a rake. The general rule was to mess about as much as you could. This was the best way of surviving, pretending to be busy.

After a three-hour wait Corporal Gómez arrived, a guy with a thin moustache and rosy cheeks. He had the peak of his cap down to his eyebrows and his boots polished to a shine. He hadn't been long at the barracks and, like many of his comrades, had signed up to escape from poverty. He opened the office door and, after clearing various things from the table, called out in a shrill voice that

11

echoed down the corridor, "Adorno! Enter."

Huidobro turned towards me at that moment, and I went into the office, not saying a word. I put the bag and the other things on the table, then looked towards my mate who was staring at the corporal. Gómez, being a good distrustful corporal, emptied out the bag and checked all the equipment was there. And as he rummaged through my things he said with a scowl, "The handkerchief is missing."

"Handkerchief? What handkerchief?"

"The handkerchief. The only handkerchief they gave you, soldier," said the corporal, preening his moustache with the top of a biro.

"Never had a handkerchief, corporal, and I tell you, it would have come in useful."

"They always give you one, along with the other kit."

"Where? But I was never given a handkerchief."

"Silence! What's this, are you doubting my word?"

"No, but I never saw any handkerchief among my stuff."

"Alright then, carry on, I'll sort you out with a handkerchief."

I knew he was basically a decent sort.

Corporal Gómez crossed off my name, which was towards the top of the list and then, without looking up from the table, said, "All the best, soldier," but this time in a tone more friendly that I hadn't expected.

"Thanks, corporal," I replied, just to keep on the right side of that insignificant little parasite.

I felt much delight at the thought that my name had begun to be wiped from every possible list. Then it was Huidobro's turn. He had no handkerchief either, but the corporal didn't even mention that. Now we had to go through that entrance gate and back to the civilian world. Every so often I turned and looked at the barracks in the middle of green parkland that stretched as far as the river. Huidobro walked straight on, not even nodding to the soldiers on duty at the gate, but I saluted everyone I met, saying I hoped to see them again soon. We walked in single file, two metres apart, along the main avenue. Once through the main gate, with our documents in our hands, I asked Huidobro once more whether he wanted to take a stroll around the centre. He made no reply yet again, and I started to feel I was somehow to blame. Maybe I was one of those he no longer wanted to see. We said goodbye with an uneasy embrace in front of the main gate.

"Let's hope we meet soon," I said. I couldn't work out why we had to leave like this. "Call me whenever you like. I'll come and see you."

Huidobro looked at me and went off, crossing the road, not looking back even once. What else could I do?

... you were the one, Fernando ... you were the one ready to shoot if an English soldier had come out from the water. You peered out to sea, your gun pointing straight ahead, just as Lieutenant Billy the Kid had shown us. Remember? I told you I wouldn't have managed to shoot ... all I wanted was to sneak away before being sent to the front line, remember? From those waters, I told you, only cannon fire could reach us ... and I had no intention of getting killed by cannon fire, in the atrocious cold of the islands. You, on the other hand, were accustomed to any climate and to any temperature, ready for anything ... I'm proud to have known you, with that face of yours painted with dark stripes of camouflage during night patrols.

I went to the station bar. I had enough money to spend a couple of hours sitting at a table. I met two regulars who talked non-stop about the World Cup. I smiled, at first, and asked polite questions, as if that place had suddenly become something else and not just somewhere you passed through; but later, when it began to turn dark and it was time to go home, I started to feel the whole weight of the barracks upon me. Strange, I thought. When I drink, I cheer up straightaway, become talkative and friendly with everyone. But that evening, after half a bottle of wine, I couldn't even smile. On top of that, there was Fernandito Huidobro who'd gone off like he had, without saying a word.

"Get a grip on yourself," I thought, "you have to start all over again now." *That's right, all over again.* But how would I cope with life in that house that opened its arms and begged me to return as soon as I could? And forget the cold, the noise of the aeroplanes, the watered-down soup.

Chapter Two

In which I return home after being discharged and my father shows me a strange grass-cutting machine he'd built while I was away

The regulars at the station bar had stopped discussing the line-up for Argentina's national team and were talking about the war. They said that one day they'd go there themselves, with a knife each, and win back the islands.

"And then," one of them said, "we'll hoist the Bolivian flag in the main square."

"Bravo, now you're talking," said the other, whose chin was all pushed to one side.

"Poor Bolivians, they've been wanting a patch of land on the coast for a hundred years."

"And what do you think, soldier boy?" they asked me as I was looking away, trying to summon the strength to return home.

"I don't think anything," I replied.

"Not even you? No one here thinks anything," said the one with the crooked chin.

I paid the barman for my half bottle of wine and made my way towards the station. After all this time, at last I could wear my jeans, my white T-shirt with Led Zeppelin faces printed on the front, and my velvet jacket. In my pockets I had my papers and my swollen fingers, red with chilblains. From the platform I could see the barracks, the great archway that separated it from the civilian world, and the four soldiers on guard with their rifles. I still don't know what had to be guarded, but they were there, dying of cold just the same.

The luminous eye of the train suddenly emerged in the distance. It was packed with people returning from work. People standing on the engine (which threw up dense black smoke), people clinging to the roofs of the wagons, people hanging from the doors, travelling on the coupling between one wagon and the next. The last arrivals fought for the two handrails on each side and for the lowest steps at the doors. As soon as the train stopped at the platform, I managed to gain ten centimetres of handrail and a pocket handkerchief of space for the tips of my toes at one corner of the last step. I was pleased to be joining that throng of people travelling from the city centre towards the suburbs. And I could indeed count myself lucky, I thought, being able to board the train during the rush hour, though in the conditions in which I was travelling, if I had fallen, I'd have no doubt broken my neck. The fifteen kilos I had lost since I left home, and my precarious position, made me feel like an eagle ready to take flight. As the train gathered speed, I started thinking back to my comrades to distract myself from the danger in which I now found myself. I remembered an evening in June. On the infantry front there were soldiers from Corrientes beating back the advance, while we were trying hard to retreat downhill. Beside me was Valenzuela, nicknamed the Duck, who was holding his jaw as he had toothache. Valenzuela the Duck was a soldier incapable of constructing a sentence without a swear word. We walked bent with the burden of the weight on our backs and our ears shattered by the din of the cannon blasts. When we stopped for a break, I offered him a cigarette. And then, because of his toothache, I told him the story about when I fell from my bike and broke one of my front teeth. The Duck pulled a face. "And what the fuck do I care about your tooth?" he yelled. "You reckon this is the right moment? I've got my own tooth that's already splitting my head open, and these fucking British carry on shooting, and you start telling me this crap?"

"All right, sorry. I was just trying to help. I thought ..."

"You don't have to think anything, dickhead. Just follow orders. Can't you see we're pulling back?"

Great! I knew perfectly well we were retreating. I also knew that *correntinos* were being killed at the front. It was hardly my fault he'd got toothache. He could have found some other way of saying he didn't want to hear the story about my front tooth, I told myself as the train journeyed on. But I had to keep up my spirits, since at that moment I was in the same situation as those poor folk who had clambered on at the last station, travelling like leaves in the wind. I wasn't afraid of falling. I'd experienced worse than falling from a moving train, though it might have been fatal. There again, you soon get used to travelling like that on your way home from work. All the same, maybe due to the wine, or knowing that I wouldn't be seeing my comrades ever again despite the promises of visits and telephone calls, I felt a oneness with all those people who were clinging to the train as it hurtled through the city. Meanwhile, bridges and railway signals of every kind flashed past at a speed I couldn't afford to underestimate.

"I love this place," I thought. "I'd feel a fool if I couldn't travel like this, hanging from a handrail."

Apart from these passing inconveniences, I could hardly grumble. I was on my way home and perhaps would never set foot in an army barracks again. I wondered if there was any way of belonging to the history of this country that wasn't fraught with risk and danger. I was learning to be an Argentine, to return home after yet another defeat. Gripping on to those ten centimetres of handrail, I could no longer feel my chilblains. After half an hour the train pulled into San Miguel station and stopped in front of a line of shops on platform two.

San Miguel was once again opening its arms to me. After months I could again walk its streets, stop below the solemn statue of Sarmiento and gaze into the illuminated shop windows. I could recognize its smells, its tooting traffic, the sound of *chamamé* music

17

blaring out from the record shops, the ramshackle buses, the looks of those crossing the Mitre and León Gallardo junction. The colours of the lights merging one into the other, forming an endless trail down the main street. It felt to me like the first time that Argentina had ever gone to war and the first time that one of its soldiers (who was also, in the words of Sergeant Alcalde, a lily-livered faggot) was returning home. What had happened in this country in the meantime? I was returning with no plan, with no intentions. All I wanted was to figure out what to do and get the burden of the past off my back.

Arriving home, fortunately, wasn't as hard as I had imagined. I banged the door twice using the knocker, as I always did when I came home without a key, and my family's hugs and kisses began immediately. I was back at last in that world to which, thanks to the imprecision of British gunsights, I'd been allowed to return. After the hugs and kisses, my father returned to the stove, stretching his hands towards the flame. My sister showed me the things she had written and drawn for me. And my mother went back to busying herself at the cooker. The evening passed slowly. Everything was still exactly as it was. After so many days spent keeping guard over the desolate landscape of those islands, the house seemed too small to hold an entire family. I wrongly imagined our neighbours, relatives, friends, everyone, would be coming that evening to celebrate my return. I too stretched my hands towards the bluish flames of the fire over which my mother had placed a pan of eucalyptus berries with a few bay leaves.

I wasn't hungry. I was happy to be with my father who took me, after a while, to the store cupboard to let me see a strange grass-cutting machine he had built with the motor from the washing machine. He had covered it with four mudguards and an orange dome in the middle. The wheels were from a plastic tractor he had once given me as a birthday present.

"It works beautifully," he said. "I'll let you see tomorrow. I haven't cut the grass on purpose."

My mother, always sceptical about my father's inventions, added that there was a risk of electric shock but all in all, she said, it worked quite well. She then came and rested her hand on my head. "When my father returned from the war, he looked half dead. I still remember. He was barely thirty and already an old man. Now, instead, it's my son who I see like that ... we haven't slept a wink all this time, you know?"

I didn't know, but I could believe it all the same. My father got up from his chair to pour two glasses of wine, one for him and a half for me. Then we sat gazing into the flames. I realized I didn't know what to say. They seemed almost like strangers. And yet I was pleased to be home at last, to warm myself in front of the stove, to smell the eucalyptus and bay leaf – although a part of me was still clinging to the cold of those islands, to my comrades. I was missing my gun, the trenches, the mud between my feet, and my homesickness.

"If you only knew what crap they've been telling us in those war bulletins," my father muttered, shaking his head.

At that moment, maybe I wouldn't have minded being back with my comrades in battle. I cleaned myself up beneath the shower. Then finally went to my room. Stretching out on the bed, I managed to sleep soundly for the first time until, around four in the morning, I was woken by the noise of a Sea Harrier passing low over our trench.

Chapter Three

On the first signs of de-Malvinization and when my grandpa came back from the war with his head still full of it

It all began around the end of June 1982. The war had finished quite some time before, and I still felt like a soldier dazed by the deafening noise of the Sea Harriers, dazed by the bombs, by the orders of the NCOs, dazed by having to repeat, "Sir, yes Sir," all the time, and so on. That war against the English had gone so deep into my gut that I just couldn't shake it off. Two months dying of cold and hunger, then returning to barracks to be told by Sergeant Alcalde that if we had shown more courage we'd have won, and the Malvinas would now belong to Argentina.

But most sad of all, when I got home, was the discovery that Grandpa Pasquale had died just a few days before. They had taken him to San Miguel Hospital on the 1st of May, the day the English had started bombing us, and when the war had turned into a physical reality. He had died on 14th June, the day of the final surrender. In that month and a half, death had held us close together – him in his final struggle, and me in the icy chill of the South. I had wanted to tell him that I too had escaped from the bombs and from hunger, and that when I saw the craters gouged out by the explosions, I remembered what he had told me. Who else would have understood, apart from him, the one who had spent two years behind barbed wire? Grandpa Pasquale, who had left Italy for the war when my grandma was pregnant with my mother and had returned when my mother was already at school. She couldn't imagine this decrepit man was her father, and hid behind mother's legs. Her mother could barely recognize him. "But it's papa," she told her daughter in that Molise dialect my grandpa hadn't heard for so long. "He's come back to you."

And on returning from those islands down there, I could see that people felt something similar to what my mother had done when she hid behind her mother's legs.

As the first troops came back, the process of de-Malvinization began and people were quite willing to be de-Malvinized. No one wanted to carry on thinking about the dead and wounded of the Malvinas, and the past was allowed to slip into the realm of oblivion. But this indifference produced the opposite effect on me and ended up Malvinizing me even more. At night I carried on dreaming of tanks, helicopters, the whistle of bullets, I dreamt that my feet, my hands were turning gangrenous or that someone was pointing the barrel of a gun at the back of my head. I didn't know which way to turn. I'd get on a bus – any bus – and as I looked out of the window I would Malvinize: I would think about Fiorito, about Cardena, about Zukovskij whom we called *el rusito*, the little Russian, and so many others who had been left behind, forgotten. Then I looked at the people around, all de-Malvinized. Sometimes the bus driver asked for my ticket and, since I didn't have one, I'd quickly get off and start walking along the roadside without stopping, then perhaps I'd take another, and if no one said anything I'd carry on to the end of the line. I'd go to the driver and say, "Look, I fell asleep, I should have got off earlier, do you mind if I go without a ticket?"

Some of them would say, "Okay, I'm leaving in half an hour, stay here." Others would say, "That's your business, boy. Be more careful next time."

"I'm back from the Malvinas," I'd say. "I've been down there and can't get sorted, so I ride about on the bus."

They'd look at me strangely. "And how many English did you kill?"

"None," I'd say. "I didn't kill any. I couldn't kill an Englishman, I wouldn't be capable."

I always got the same reply. "You want to scrounge a lift, and you couldn't even manage to kill an Englishman?"

People didn't de-Malvinize themselves intentionally, they just wanted to forget. Certain things happen like that, for no reason. Some didn't want to think any more about it. But others remained anchored to those fateful days and thought that climbing onto a bus that took them to the end of the line or drinking a beer was the best way of following the flow of events. Once I even went as far as Casa Rosada to look up at its balconies and recall the speeches of President Galtieri when he declared that the whole population of Argentina would fight to the last drop of blood until those islands were taken back. And those people, I thought, who had cheered in the hope of seeing our blue and white flag flying over those islands, now carry on their de-Malvinized lives with no regard for the many who died down there.

I needed to get the war out of my head. Sometimes I would let off steam by writing down a load of stuff against Margaret Thatcher, against Menéndez and against that whole hierarchy of dickheads. And then I'd go to Tío Pablo's and stay till closing time. The barman would come with his squint eyes and ask whether I proposed to settle the bill.

"I'll bring you part of it tomorrow. I've got to go and pick up my Aunt Albertina's pension," I told him.

Beer reconciled me to reality. Then, half asleep on the table, I heard a voice whispering in my ear. "Alberto! Eh! It's time to shift your ass and start doing something. It's late."

"Late? Late for what?" I asked.

"You don't want to go through your whole life doing nothing? Come on, shift that ass. What does it take to start doing something? Move yourself!" it whispered again.

*

22

One day, to keep the voice happy, I went to the offices of *La Voz* to look for Fatty Beto, who was the chief editor at that time, and didn't wear a wig as he does now, but combed his hair with infinite care over his bald patch, starting from the left ear before arriving at the other side of his head. When the wind blew, it lifted his hair, and he immediately flattened it with the palm of his hand. He walked about with those few tufts of hair on his head. At Tío Pablo's they called him the Botticelli of the combover. That day when I went to see him, I told him I'd like to write a piece about the 16th June, my last day on the Malvinas, and to describe what it was like when we were on the *Canberra*. I wanted to write about what it was like to be a prisoner of war because, as I told Fatty Beto, I never imagined the English would treat us with such respect.

"You'll never manage to write things like that," Fatty Beto told me, fixing me with those inexpressive eyes.

"And why won't I?"

"Precisely because you experienced them, you'll never manage to write anything on the war."

"What do you mean?"

"Forget it, read Fogwill instead."

"You don't earn a single *peso* reading other writers."

"Why, because you want to get paid as well?"

"And who's going to pay my bill at Tío Pablo's, the government?"

But he kept on saying I'd do better reading Fogwill.

"Has he written about the war, this Fogwill?"

"Sure."

"Well then?"

"But why write about what people want to forget? It's over, you've got to look forward, we have too many dead to bury as it is."

How could I explain to Fatty Beto that I couldn't forget, that I'd been dreaming at night about helicopters and bombs for the last two years?

"It's all over, there's no point droning on like an old soldier."

"But who was I fighting?" I wondered. "I didn't see a single Englishman at the front during that fucking war! They only came out when we surrendered, those bastards; the English kept well clear of the *gauchos*; if I'd seen one of them, maybe I'd have fired, but the English used to send the Gurkhas into the front line."

That's who the English were, the princelings of the crown. When they got back to England, there was nothing they had to deal with, they didn't have their heads stuffed full of the war, no de-Malvinization, not like me. After all this time, I still couldn't make sense of it all.

My grandpa also had his head stuffed full when he came back home from the war and had to get over it. And in the evening, he'd shut himself in the local taberna with other ex-soldiers and drink red wine: he couldn't avoid it. He'd return home drunk rotten. My grandma waited for him at the door and helped put him to bed. She kept telling him they couldn't stay there dying of hunger in the Italian mountains in the snow, she was tired of smuggling tobacco from one town to the next and watching her children grow up in poverty. She decided the only way out of the general mess after the war was to go to America (where her older brother lived) and start all over again.

"Lots of people are going to America," she told my grandpa one day. "They're comfortably off, there's work, there's everything."

And my grandpa, who couldn't come to terms with what had happened, asked, "So what shall we do?"

"We'll sell the house, go off by ship, that's what we'll do."

"And then if something happens?"

"What do you want to happen?"

"I don't know, our life is here, in Italy, we were born here."

"Ha ... life, country ... your life, you don't have one ... what life is it going off drinking every day?"

My grandpa thought it over, that same day, and before going to bed had made a decision. "I'll tell you what, Alfunsí. We'll go as well, down to America."

They sold their house and set off for Argentina in 1950 with three children and five cardboard suitcases. The port of Naples at that time was swarming with immigrants. They sailed on the *Francesco Morosino* and after eighteen days reached Buenos Aires. When they stopped over at Dakar, my mother stroked the black frizzy hair of some African children who looked at her and smiled, hoping for some money. In Argentina, my grandpa soon got over the war and built himself a house at Don Torquato, a district full of Italians and with dirt roads; that was another problem but at least, he said, there were no Germans. That was life. He had the comfort of his family, and a few years later he'd be surrounded by a swarm of young grandchildren who would kick his flowers and tomatoes and pull plums off his trees to throw at each other. He used to shake his head and watch us from a distance.

"What are you worrying about," my grandma Alfonsina used to say, "for the sake of two or three tomatoes?"

This, in the end, was what he wanted, to grow old and play the grandfather, for he hadn't been a father during wartime. Things had been too tough. He hadn't had the time or the energy. But he felt comfortable in the role of grandfather, even though he was in Argentina, far from his hometown, his hair turning grey and sprouting from his ears and nostrils.

And now I was about to travel back in the opposite direction. But this turn of events was thanks to my grandpa who on 30th April 1982, my birthday, had just begun to get ill and had left me a gold chain for when I came back. My grandpa knew his turn had come. He had seen the face of death too many times and knew that this time it was for real. He thought that one day, by selling the gold chain, I could go back and see his country, his people, and the place where he had lived. I was the one he wanted to make the final return he had never managed to make. And so, a couple of years later, I would see that country through his eyes, would touch the worn frontages of the houses with his hands and maybe hear the distant voices, half a century old, that still called out, "It's Pasquale! Pasquale is back."

And I, in the body of my grandpa, would reply, "Of course I'm back, did you think I was going to let those Germans kill me?"

And then I would walk, with his legs, along those narrow lanes as far as the door of his house and for a short while I'd become that old man, racked with rheumatism, who looked at me shaking his head as I had been kicking his tomatoes. I'd find myself with his relatives, dead and living, and they would all hug me and say, "O Pasquà! You're back from America, Pasquà. What's going on, there in America? Is it cold like here? And Nanní, how's Nanní? And Carmelí? Tell us, tell us."

And I am there, still in the body of my grandpa, telling them, "All is well ... all's well ..." But later I would become his grandson once more and would hear those voices which, between their words of greeting, would say, "Send our love to Mamma Costanza. And our love to Grandma Alfonsina and tell her that here, in Riccia, we're always thinking of her and always praying for the soul of Pasquale, may God bless him, our poor Pasquale!"

And then I would leave them, and my grandpa would thank me for going to see his people, and I would give him back his eyes, his legs, his voice, and he would go off in peace along a dark stone-paved lane until he merged into his shadow which flickered along the town walls.

Chapter Four

In which, as a prisoner of war, I board the English ship that takes me back to the mainland

The only real souvenir I had of the Malvinas, apart from an undershirt and a pair of woollen socks, was a small forty-page exercise book with black cover. There was no writing inside, apart from an inscription on the first page made by an English soldier called John Smith: "This notebook is for my friend Alberto Adorno, in memory of this stupid war."

I kept it by my bed, and in the evening, on my return home, I'd close myself in my room and would leaf through it, knowing I'd find nothing else but horizontal lines. It was enough though to hear the rustle of the pages, and that light waft of air they created before my eyes, to recall the day when I finally came back from the islands.

It was the morning of 16th June. We were walking in single file along the roadside. A large grey cloud over barren desolate expanses. The cold was so intense that my feet were numb. I was driven only by the urge to get away from the place, an urge that forced me to follow the footsteps of my comrades advancing in silence towards the port. The English escorted us in their vehicles. It didn't take much to realize we were not at all prepared for a military campaign like that. You could see that the British were disciplined and expert from the way they behaved but above all they were conscious of having gone to war. We, on the other hand, were a disorderly bunch who couldn't even walk straight, were cold and hungry, and had one thought buzzing around in our heads: to get home. Nothing else. On the march towards the port, I was one of those who had to stop every so often, who had to grip hold of their ankles, let four or five soldiers pass, then carry on in line. A month or so earlier I had been to hospital for the same reason: frostbitten toes. A condition well known among Argentine soldiers, known as *pie de trinchera*, "trench foot". But now that we were about to board ship, I didn't want anyone to see I was having difficulty walking, I was afraid they'd send me back to hospital and leave me there till God knows when. The lights of the port glinted in the distance through the sleet. No one knew for sure where they would take us, but it wasn't difficult to figure out that the lights beyond the port were those of a large ship that would be returning us to the mainland.

The port was small, and Argentine soldiers were boarding several English boats along the quay.

"Before boarding you have to leave everything behind," we heard it murmured.

"Everything, leave everything you have," repeated Captain Correas, as he moved away from the line and strode towards the head of the troops. And, as he was ordering us to leave whatever we had, an English soldier approached to ask him his rank.

"Captain," said Captain Correas, eying the soldier with an air of defiance, as though he had seen all his power suddenly disintegrate. Correas was a reliable sort, one who had those qualities which stirred admiration among fellow soldiers: a sort of superstar warrior, though he'd never fought before.

The English soldier told him to move away from the troop, pointing to a small group of officers awaiting allocation. First, though, he told him to remove his stripes.

"So, this is it!" was my first thought as I watched the captain's bewilderment.

The captain left, looking annoyed. He wasn't used to taking orders from a foreign soldier. The whole troop turned to watch him as he walked away. I wasn't sure whether to feel pleased about what had happened, after all he was a decent chap, but I felt a satisfaction that the hierarchy, of which the army was so proud, had been turned upside down, and that now, at the end, those at the bottom of the ladder were first to leave.

English soldiers at the entrance to the quay were searching all those about to board the boats. I was leaving those islands at last! I was ready to face defeat without too much disappointment, just as long as I could get back to Buenos Aires.

In my pocket I had two bars of *Mantecol* which I'd just been given, and ate them there and then, with a certain greed (an empty stomach, so far as I know, is the least tolerable form of emptiness, assuming there are others). Then I hid the small book I'd had with me since I first went into the army in the outside pocket of my trousers. It was the first edition of a collection of poems by my friend Carlitos, and I swear I would never have left those islands without it. It was something I cherished, though I found the poetry somewhat obscure.

The English soldier conducting the search looked fairly severe. He wore his helmet loose and seemed to enjoy grabbing anything that anyone was carrying and throwing it onto a pile of stuff a few yards away. He looked like someone I'd seen many times before, though at that very moment I couldn't remember who – I needed to re-learn how to connect thoughts to objects. In front of me was Revueltas, a soldier famous for his crabs. He had a pair of air force binoculars hidden under his jacket which he wanted to take home as a war trophy. As soon as the searching officer found them, Revueltas, though not knowing a word of English, tried explaining in his Castilian drawl that he had found the binoculars in a hut at the airport and wanted to take them back with him. Waving his arms around like a salami vendor, he explained that he wanted the binoculars so he could surprise thieves climbing over the wall of his house and then, perhaps, throw stones at them. It's impossible to imagine what the Englishman could have made of Revueltas's story, but he snatched the binoculars all the same and threw them onto the nearby pile. Then, pointing at the sea, he said, "Carry on!"

I moved slowly towards the officer, still not sure that they would let me onto the boats. The English, from the little I could understand, were unpredictable. Once I reached him, he began frisking me, my arms, my ribs, around my waist. Then suddenly he stopped at my trouser pocket and made a sign that was impossible to misinterpret. I pulled out Carlitos's book. The English soldier took it from me, casually opened it and, as he glanced at the back cover, asked me in the same tone he might have used to order me before a firing squad, "Who is he?"

I looked yet again at the photograph of Carlitos lighting up a cigarette and gave him the only answer I was able to give in his language: "He is… my friend."

The soldier flicked through the book again, then did something which, even today, I can't be sure what to make of: he let it slip from his hands so that it fell to the ground. We stared at each other for a second. My sense of uncertainty was enormous. He hadn't thrown the book onto the pile of confiscated objects, nor had he had the decency to return it to me. I didn't know what to make of it. Should I leave it there? Or pick it up? I bent down, still fixing him in the eye. I expected to be kicked in the teeth, or that he would trample the cover. But he did nothing, watching me as I picked up the book and moved towards the quay, swept along by the line of soldiers in front of me, with the book in my hand. I didn't even have the courage to turn round, fearing that he'd call me back or that I'd be hit with the butt of a gun. I put the book back in my outside pocket.

A few minutes later I was being tended by two nurses from the International Red Cross. They asked if I felt well, and I said yes.

"Never felt better."

They were in no mood for jokes – you could tell that from their look. Nor was I, for that matter. They then asked me to open my mouth, to stick out my tongue.

"Now let us see your hands. All right, turn them over. Now lift your jacket."

I felt the cold stethoscope against my chest and finally, as I was about to leave, one of the nurses, with blondish hair and buck teeth, took me by the arm. "Hold on, why are you limping?"

"It's nothing," I said. "My feet hurt, I'm cold, hungry, tired ... I want to board that bloody ship and get straight out of here."

The nurse said nothing, just nodded, and I climbed into a small boat, helped by an Englishman. I couldn't put any weight on the sole of my foot. As I looked back towards the far entrance of the quay, I caught sight for the last time of the officer who had searched me: "Dylan Thomas!"

That was who he looked like!

There was a photo of him on the cover of a book I had recently bought: Dylan Thomas sitting with a glass in his hand, against a completely black background. This one looked just like him, with the only difference that he didn't have the face of someone who could down eighteen whiskies in succession, and write: *I've had 18 straight whiskies, I think that's the record.* You could see perfectly well that he was a limp British prick who enjoyed playing tough with us.

We set off in those boats towards the ship and, through the mist, a little later, the *SS Canberra* loomed into sight in all its magnificence. The closer we got, the more it grew in length and height. Yes, that vast ocean liner was beyond every dream! This was the ship that had interrupted a Mediterranean cruise and returned home to take on board more than two thousand marines; the same ship that, according to the Argentine military bulletins, ought to have been at the bottom of the ocean, sunk by our missiles. And yet it was there waiting for us, ready to take us back to *terra firma.* When we entered the bowels of that great liner, the English guards led us up a long series of carpeted stairways, to a great lounge. It was quite unsuitable for transporting prisoners of war. Trampling over the brightly coloured carpet in my dirty shoes made me feel even more filthy and despicable. Over the loudspeakers, in broken Spanish, they reeled out the rules we would have to follow – mealtimes and various precautions. I soon realized that our treatment would be kinder than what we had received from our own superiors. They searched us a second time. They wanted to be sure we weren't carrying any dangerous items. They even made us remove our shoelaces in case someone got it into their heads to commit some heroic act after our defeat. Maybe they were overestimating us. It was obvious that no one would have attempted suicide once they had managed to board the ship. With no laces, however, I felt lighter. My feet were still hurting, but I preferred to hold back my pain until I reached Buenos Aires.

The soldier conducting the search seemed a decent type, and not as strict as Dylan Thomas. This time, the idea of having to give up Carlitos's book didn't strike me as so tragic. It was his first book, published that same year, and he still had plenty of copies to give away. Fortunately, though, the guard didn't even notice. Then they took down our details, gave us an identification number, a glass of tomato juice, and the chance to have a shower. After two months, we could look at our naked bodies in a mirror and say hello once more to our dicks, shrivelled in the cold. The war had sapped all our strength, and we now all looked the same, and even difficult to tell apart: we were haggard and full of dark blotches. I felt rather ashamed to see myself appear so different. I could see my collar bones, my ribs, my emaciated stomach, my long neck. We were no longer what we had been before, we looked in fact as if we had never been anybody. They also gave us razors for shaving, and there was general laughter at the sight of our superiors who had managed to sneak in among the lower ranks and were busy removing their tell-tale moustaches, to be treated like us, like those at the bottom of the ladder. Their military dignity, after that shave, had been reduced to that of a bare, bristleless mouth.

Next day the ship had begun to move on the water, you could feel it, and it was a pleasure to know that sooner or later we would be sailing far away from that dull greyness that enveloped the island. Then, after two or three blasts of the siren, we started to head off towards the mainland. From the portholes we could see the beaches and the first hills that rose up behind the small town which for seventy-five days had been Puerto Argentino (and now returned to Port Stanley, as it had been before).

The ship took two days to reach the mainland: it moved slowly on the grey southern waters that were pushing us west. From the deck of the ship, I could feel the water rise and fall, surging ceaselessly back and forth, in continual agitation. And we, prisoners of war, standing like statues, waiting anxiously for land.

On the second day I was sitting, casually reading Carlitos's book, when an English soldier came up and asked what I was reading.

"A book of poetry," I replied, and showed it to him.

The soldier took the book, flicked through it, then pointed to the title on the front cover. "*El grito de la langosta*. What is a *langosta*?" he asked.

It made me smile to hear an English soldier reading my language, with those guttural sounds I had never heard before, and that way of rounding the consonants. It was the first time I'd ever had a conversation with a foreigner.

"*La langosta? La langosta* is an insect that eats everything, green, strange," I replied, accompanying each word with gestures.

"Locust?" smiled the soldier. "Yes, locust," he continued, clapping one hand with the palm of the other. I think he found the sound of that word quite funny. *Langosta, langosta.*

"Yes, locust!" and I too started laughing without knowing why.

He was reading and laughing. Then he took my shoulder as if he'd found some magic formula. "*The Locust's Outcry*?"

"What?"

"*The Locust's Outcry*?" he repeated, pointing to the title.

"Er … maybe".

I hadn't understood, but it sounded good all the same. Then I realized the soldier wanted to keep Carlitos's book as a souvenir, and I was pleased to thank anyone for the journey that was taking me back to *terra firma*. I wanted to give it to him, not least because it was at risk of being snatched by one of my comrades who, now the war had ended, were filching all they could find, just like locusts.

"You can keep it, if you like."

The English soldier looked at me with a smile. He'd understood straightaway. "Is it for me?"

"Yes, for *tu*."

"Oh, thank you!" he said, giving me three or four pats on the back.

Then he asked my name, and to write it inside the book. Finally, he told me to wait there for him – he would be back with something in return.

And as I sat there, thinking about going back home, and so many other things that now seemed so distant, though only two months had passed, there was a sudden general explosion of excitement among the prisoners. A cheer rose, people were pointing to a small speck far away on the straight line of the horizon. "Argentina! Yes, Puerto Madryn!"

It was quite a sight to see those blotchy-skinned faces, with their dark sunken cheeks, blue lips and skin ingrained with dirt, shouting and leaping for joy, pointing to that strip on the horizon, so thin and faint as to seem unreal. At that moment we were all hugging each other and yelling, "We've arrived! We've arrived!"

And I thought to myself, "Fuck Margaret Thatcher and all the English! Fuck the islands, fuck the *Canberra* and its British luxury! Fuck the Argentine army, its lieutenants, its colonels and all the mothers who gave birth to them! Fuck weapons, hunger and minefields!"

The English, who were sticklers for discipline, told us to return to the lounge and keep calm. But our heads weren't clear enough for us to follow their orders to the letter. I was going downstairs towards the lounge when I felt someone take hold of my arm. I turned and saw the soldier who had been searching for me.

"And what does this Englishman want from me, now?"

"This is for you," he said. He pushed an exercise book into my hand. I opened it straight away. On the first page was written: *This notebook is for my friend Alberto Adorno, in memory of this stupid war. John Smith.*

"John Smith!" I said, hugging him in thanks. "*Thank you*, John Smith. But now I'm going back to Buenos Aires, John Smith, to my home. Enjoy the islands you've won. Those islands you've won, I don't want them any longer. In fact, you know what, John Smith? I don't give a shit for those fucking Falklands of yours ... and I hope shit is the only thing that grows there ... my friend ..."

"I wish you good luck!"

"Perhaps one day we'll see each other again and we'll go for a drink of Scotch, what do you say, English soldier John Smith?"

"Yes," he said smiling.

I carried on down the stairs, dragged along by the multitude who bounded from one step to another. Outside, the grey waters of the Atlantic were pushing us onward ... and in the meantime I pressed my hands tightly together, as though I wanted to grip that absent rifle I had left back there in the middle of a pile of weapons.

Chapter Five

Which tells of my war training in the first month of military service and when Lieutenant Colonel Zanaya announces that we are at war with the English

Ramiro belonged to an artillery battalion that had fought on Mount Longdon. He hated the English since he was a child – he hated them because he hated invaders. At school he had been taught that in 1806, or thereabouts, the English had invaded Buenos Aires and the people had managed to defeat them by throwing boiling oil over them from the rooftops. This made him proud to be Argentine. And yet, when he ended up prisoner on the *Canberra*, he was happy to accept an English offer of whisky or chocolate. He said all the English looked like podgy kids, all pale with red cheeks and blue eyes. But then, when one of his mates suggested his girlfriend might fancy going to bed with one of those podgy kids, he turned serious and felt more of a prisoner than ever before.

"Those shits," he would say, "why don't they go to war in their own country? Haven't they got anything better to do?"

When Ramiro grew angry, he became serious and we laughed behind his back; but when he laughed, it made us feel rather sad. He came from the city of Comodoro Rivadavia where he worked as a car body repairer. Two years after returning from the war he had a daughter with the girl he had always lived with. Everyone who knew him said he was a model father. In 1992, precisely ten years after his return, he wrote a note: *I swore to defend the flag and I did, but no one defended me.*

That same evening, he left the city and waited on the tracks, with his arms spread open, for the next train.

We had finished up in an incomprehensible world, where small things became so essential that everything brought us to despair, like that time when Black Pelé shot a young goose that was paddling by the seashore, then took off his shoes and trousers to go and get it and nearly had a heart attack from the cold.

"How can you let a goose get away like that?" he said, as the current carried him off.

Watching Black Pelé turning purple and shaking like a leaf made me laugh somewhat, thinking how ridiculous it was to find myself fighting among those rocks on an empty stomach.

By the end of the war, I still had those hundred bullets they'd given me at the start. I'd used about ten of them, but not at the English. I had shot at animals for food. I managed to hit one – one animal. Black Pelé was much better than me: he would aim at something and hit it, and if he didn't, he'd carry on until he did.

As a child I had played football more than once with Black Pelé and now, quite by chance, we found ourselves in combat together. He was built like a midfielder, straight black hair, dark eyes, broken nose and the wild stare of someone destined to fight every day to survive. He always played football barefoot – he had only one pair of shoes which he kept for going to work. I, on the other hand, had a pair specially for football but every time I tackled him it was me who ended up hurt. I think he did it on purpose, to show he could do better than me even without shoes. And he succeeded. He said there was also Indian blood in his black veins – he was proud of that. But we were now two hungry soldiers with no blood or energy. He was respected by everyone in the patrol, though we considered him a strange type and somewhat unpredictable. Or perhaps we respected him because he was a strange and unpredictable type. It was rare for Black Pelé to complain about anything. If there was a goose to be shot and he had to go and get it in the middle of icy waters, he was the first to step forward; if a two-metre hole had to be dug, he'd take the spade and he'd dig a two-metre hole. He was a man who was made for war and for football but, unfortunately, he had neither a gun that shot straight nor a pair of boots. And when in the evening we sat down for a rest, he'd sit to one side sucking a blade of grass. He was the sort who, if he'd got hold of a bottle of wine, he'd have drunk it all in one go and would then have gone off to fight all by himself against the English.

He didn't much like being called Black Pelé – he preferred being called by his own name, or just Black. At that time there was Maradona, and to call someone Pelé was like belittling him. He didn't want to be second to anyone, but we carried on calling him like that, Black Pelé.

The month of military training was carried out at the El Palomar training camp, between March and April 1982. The camp was a vast wooded area in front of the military airport and the war training I had to do involved cleaning and loading my gun, knowing how to wield a knife in the event of hand-to-hand combat, and crawling along the ground until my elbows and knees bled. We also had to learn order and discipline, how to shit all together in ditches and throw quicklime over it, not to light cigarettes at night in case the enemy spotted us, to talk quietly, and to pray, always to pray, and to obey. In other words, they were preparing us to fight a nineteenth-century war. I went to the shooting range twice in all – that was enough to become a soldier, they said. On the first occasion I shot five bullets. On the second time I shot three since there weren't any more. I got nowhere near the target. They said it was a question of touch.

"I, for example," my companion explained, "to hit the target, I already know I have to point more to the right of centre and then, yes, perhaps I'll get a hit."

But Captain Correas told us to keep calm, because with a bit of courage we'd see off those British with a good kick up the ass. "Didn't we win the World Cup in '78?" he said. "Now we'll win the war as well!"

During that month of war training, we slept in narrow tents pitched on muddy ground. Above the tents were big eucalyptus trees where an enormous army of green parakeets had nested. Early in the morning, when the sun came up, there was a mad swarming of parakeets annoyed by our presence. Towards evening the flocks gathered around the trees and, as soon as darkness fell, they went quiet in their night refuges. But when daylight returned, they started squawking all over again. They had long pointed wings and always flew in a straight line with quick flaps of the wing. Looking at them they seemed frightened that at any moment they might fall to the ground. It was the most beautiful time of the day, waking up at dawn and hearing the parakeets overhead.

One April morning, over the din of the parakeets, we heard a group of people by the edge of the road on the other side of the wire fence which divided our training camp from the civilian world. There were twenty or thirty people with flags and drums. They were shouting in unison: "Argentina! Argentina! Argentina!" No one could explain the reason for all this cheering. We thought they had come to celebrate some football victory. The NCOs stopped us from going up to the fence.

"What's going on, sergeant? That bunch of people there, aren't they trying to tell us something?" I asked as they ordered me away.

"What is this? We're the ones who ask the questions here. Who are you to ask questions, soldier?"

"Nothing, sergeant! I was just wondering. I saw those people with flags ... it seemed a bit unusual, sergeant."

"Aha! The recruit thinks it's a bit unusual, wants me to explain?"

"If that's possible, sergeant."

"Why sure, and how does he want it explaining to him? Does he want us to go for a coffee so that I can tell him nice and quietly? Well, soldier?"

"Nothing, sergeant. If that's how things are then I'd prefer not to know, sergeant. It's not important."

"Aha! Now the soldier doesn't want to know. For the soldier, it no longer matters why those people are there."

"Exactly sergeant, quite right."

"Stand to attention, soldier! I want discipline! I've never liked curious sorts like you, do you know that?"

"No, sergeant. I didn't, but now I do, sergeant."

"Silence! And now get out of here quick and don't let me see you again!" And he gave me a kick in the ass for asking questions.

I realized, in effect, that I'd formulated a question with a sentence that was too long, and the sergeant, apart from not wanting to give explanations, didn't have the patience to stop there listening to me.

That same evening, we assembled on the barracks' football ground. More than five hundred recruits standing in line in the rain. After waiting half an hour, Lieutenant Colonel Ernesto Zanaya arrived, accompanied by a military escort that preceded him to the centre of the field.

"A…ttention!" shouted Sergeant Alcalde, bolt upright on the centre line; at that moment there was a single sound of hands against sides and all the recruits looked in one direction.

Zanaya was a rather stocky man, with thick hair and a moustache that set him apart him from the civilian world. Like all men of his rank, he harboured a great resentment towards everything that represented society and life outside the barracks. He wore high boots and a leather belt with a gun holster hooked to it. The rain made him look harsh, a man of few words. After a series of sharp glances, he started off with a long rambling speech about the role of the army in defending the country. Finally, when no one was expecting it, he announced that we were at war with the English. "The Argentine army has retaken what has always belonged to it and you have been chosen today to defend it. You ought to feel proud to be players in this historic event …Together we shall all support this war – those who go to the front as well as those who remain here."

Finally, he added that a fleet of enemy ships would shortly be reaching the Malvinas. The British government, with all diplomatic negotiations at an end, had decided to declare war against us.

"And we'll show them just who they're dealing with!"

Zanaya had very clear ideas but seemed a person who was far from sober. I wondered what was so profoundly Argentine about those inhospitable islands to justify an armed operation; those islands were so irrelevant to me that I didn't even remember that the English called them the Falklands, as the lieutenant colonel had told us. I contented myself with a smile, seeing that we weren't supposed to know anything else. I ought to have realized from the very start that those pips that decorated Zanaya's shoulder concealed the secret of our whole country: a collection of myths and unbearable disappointments.

Before ending he asked for the greatest respect to our flag, which we should defend to the death as a symbol of our identity. "These are the blue and white colours that give meaning to our life," Zanaya said. He had obviously been drinking.

One of his retinue sheltered him with his umbrella from the rain, while it continued to pour down, soaking all of us on the football pitch. From the very beginning it was clear who would have to defend the flag to the death, who would be destined to die of cold, and who not. He ended with another sharp glance along the front row, and left the field between two lines of soldiers, all standing stock-still. Sergeant Alcalde remained bolt upright with his chin drawn in a position of attention and, as the lieutenant colonel passed before him, his right hand sprang up with precision,

41

bringing his fingertips to his temple. Finally, turning to the first row under his command, he ordered, "Eeeea ... sy! Fall out and return to your tents!"

All through the night I kept thinking about those people who'd come all the way to the boundary fence to cheer us on and encourage us to fight. If I'd known earlier, I'd have lobbed a few stones at them.

Some of us laughed incredulously about the war that was about to take place, others were ready to arm themselves straightaway to defend our wounded pride, but there were others who weren't laughing and had no wish to fight.

From that day the war began to assume the features of Lieutenant Colonel Zanaya – a war with a black moustache, run by alcoholics.

They had us crawling along the ground, knowing that we'd soon be hearing the constant whistle of bullets over our heads. Everything we did was aimed at coping with the possibility we might find ourselves in front of the enemy. And yet I'd never had any enemies. It had to be some mistake, the lieutenant colonel's alcoholic delirium. Could the English come here and butcher us for a few remote islands stuck in the Atlantic? What was the point of it? Why did we have to fight them right now? But there again, hadn't we been taught at school that the islands were ours? It couldn't get worse than this. Now everyone was talking about the organization of the English fleet, about the Gurkhas, the guns, and the possibility of surrender, but when all speculation was put aside, the only certain thing that still had any semblance of reality was us, dressed in our camouflage jackets holding our guns. Everything else slipped out of hand and only worsened our fears.

"Do you know where these shits are sending us?" I asked my tent-mate, who lived in some remote shack way up north in Santiago del Estero and had never been away from home, except for military service.

"No," he said.

"You don't have a grandpa or anyone who's fought in a war?"

"Not me. You?"

"I have, yes."

"And what does he say about war?"

"Nothing, he's not the sort to talk about it."

"They say that maybe Russian aircraft carriers are coming, with four thousand soldiers ready to land on the Malvinas," he said in his sing-song voice, between long pauses.

"And you think that's better?"

"I don't know, but the Russians are pretty tough."

For my *santiagueño* comrade, the army was one of the world's many sacred things. He had a high sense of respect and if someone had decided he had to take up arms, then he was ready to do so without a fuss. And I wondered, meanwhile, how our lives could possibly depend on the drunken schemes of our superiors. I didn't feel ready to spill my blood for those islands down there. And yet war was getting closer every day and the English fleet was steadily advancing across the waters of the Atlantic.

"So you reckon the Russians are tough."

"Yes, but we're the tougher ones."

Chapter Six

Which tells of various things and makes several leaps in time: from the call-to-arms to when, down in the Malvinas, I see a stray sheep step on an exposed anti-personnel mine

It was a sunny, cloudless day. From the bus stop I could see a large hangar crowded with conscripts. I had no idea what awaited me in that hangar and what would be my ultimate destination, but I walked on ahead. Military service was supposed to be just an interlude, a chance to get my hair shaved so that it would re-grow with added vigour. Once inside, a little man who looked like a corporal pointed me to the long line of conscripts. I joined the queue and, after waiting half an hour, sat on the ground beside other recruits who had arrived earlier. There was a lot of talk about our future destination. But no one knew where we'd be sent. Spending a year in the city certainly wasn't the same thing as spending a year of your life a thousand kilometres from home in who knows what god-forsaken barracks in Patagonia. It was a wasted year wherever you happened to end up, and that was what my future comrades thought. Every so often someone with the face of a zombie went past carrying some registers under his arm and clouted me on the back of the head, just like that, for no reason. I had no idea what he wanted. One, two, three clouts. "What's going on, why me?" I wondered. I couldn't say anything, I had to learn to accept it, this was clear from the beginning. My future comrades laughed, and after a while I was laughing too. But after yet another clout I turned round, just to let him know he was hitting me even harder.

"Come on, straight line, we're not in a marketplace," he said, ignoring me.

To be quite honest, I'd never sat on the ground in a marketplace – I did it that day only because others had already done it before me. And there again, I was tired of that bruising on my head. I got up in the same way that anyone else who cared about their future would have done, but after a while I sat down on the ground again. When he came back, the zombie gave me another clout behind the head and made me get up once again.

"I see you haven't understood about discipline yet! Jump up! Come on, start jumping up, up ... Higher, higher still!" shouted the officer in front of the rest of those around me who had all stood up together, just in case. And I jumped as high as I could like a moron, and they all laughed at me jumping. After a few minutes he stopped me and ordered me to lift my arms as high as I could.

"And now," he said, "scratch the bollocks of St Peter. Come on, recruit, scratch the bollocks of St Peter, I said, quick!" I didn't understand what this scratching the bollocks of St Peter meant, and I looked at him with a certain embarrassment. The NCO showed me a gesture with the hands, and I immediately understood what he wanted from me. I spent half an hour with my arms up in the air moving my fingers here and there, as if I were scratching the saint's holy attributes.

A line of lorries was in front of the hangar, ready to take us to our destination. Out of one of the lorries stepped the conscript group-leader with the number eighty-three, a large puffed-up man, dark-skinned, with eyes at half-mast and epaulettes on his jacket from which I couldn't make out whether he was a corporal, a sergeant or what. But he ordered us to get in line. I was still scratching the bollocks of Saint Peter and, when he saw me, came up and gave me another clout to the back of my head. "What are you doing, you idiot?"

"I've been told I've got to scratch St Peter's bollocks, sir."

45

"Who told you?"

"Someone who was here, sir."

"Someone who was here? What are you talking about?"

"Sorry, sir."

"That's enough. Stand in line before I take hold of *your* balls!" And with a clout that was harder than all the others he put me, literally, into line.

Then he began the rollcall. He too swaggered about in charge of all those recruits who had no idea where they were going to end up – whether north, south, east or west. He glared at us and if anyone looked him in the eye, he'd get a few clouts round the back of the head. Clouting was much in vogue among those zombies. After a two-hour wait they ordered us onto the lorries. We were there up to our necks. We were entering that limbo world in which everything lost its dignity. It would have been useless to ask where they were taking us. "To the asshole of the world," they'd have replied.

"The asshole of the world?"

"Yes, you two-bit recruit, the asshole of the world."

And I remember (for I remember every tiny detail of that episode, as if I were looking at it through a microscope) that in that asshole of the world, down in the far Atlantic, there was a sheep, a small lost sheep. It was wandering undisturbed into the minefield, beyond where we were positioned. Every so often it stopped, nibbled a shrub, then quietly carried on. The *Santiagueño* called out at it from a distance. "Here, little lamb."

But the lamb pretended not to hear. The *Santiagueño* nudged me. "What a cute little lamb, eh! Look at all that wool! And those hips."

"What are you talking about?"

"Nothing, nothing," said the *Santiagueño* as he kept calling out to it even louder. "Come here, little lamb, where are you going all by yourself? There are mines out there, don't do anything silly."

The sheep didn't seem to hear, minding its own business. It flexed its legs, raised its head, sniffed the air. Then it started to walk, taking tiny steps, faster and faster, until in the end it was running headlong towards the minefield.

"Stop, little sheep, stop! Hey, where are you off to?" shouted the *Santiagueño*, but the sheep, being a stupid animal, felt more and more threatened. In the end, it ran straight into the minefield, and stepped on the exposed head of an antipersonnel mine. We saw it thrown into the air like a puppet being shot from the mouth of a cannon. The *Santiagueño* held his head in his hands and started crying.

"These islands are cursed! I want to get out of here. Come on, Alberto, stab my foot with a bayonet; do it when I'm not looking, when I'm asleep, take the bayonet and do it, stab me in the foot, the leg, on the arm, wherever you want, just enough to put me out of action," said the soldier, who was stuck there in a trench with a mortar that dated back to the 1940s and which only worked if you hit the firing pin with a hammer. "I want to end up in the infirmary, so they'll fucking well send me home. They're going to kill us all here, you understand?"

"Listen, you know what you have to do? When they serve you cornmeal, piss on it and eat it, that's what you do if you want to get hepatitis; and with hepatitis they'll send you back for sure. I'm not going to stab you, don't even think of it."

"I don't want to go into the hereafter dressed like this, anyway."

"There's nothing else to wear, unless you want to risk asking a civilian for some clothes."

"Have you ever seen a dead body dressed like this?"

"No, the only dead body I've ever seen was Perón. A neighbour of ours took me to the funeral. Two days queuing to see him inside a glass case, looking like a statue."

"All dead bodies lying in glass cases look like statues," continued the soldier. "That's because there you don't see death. I saw a neighbour who died of cancer of the liver, but you saw nothing of the cancer. You saw the dead body and that was it. But in war, people seem to die more, because you see what they die of, and you say: holy shit, this is death."

We shivered with cold. Ten degrees below zero. Feet soaking and stomach gripped with hunger. We found it hard to understand what was going on, the bombardments, the cries of the wounded. We were destined to become one big nothing, that's the truth. We rarely thought about the future; after all, what was the point? But there was still one of us who used to say that if he got out of there he'd go and live in the mountains and grow old up there. He'd learn to play the guitar and would never want to hear any more talk of work and war. There was another who said that if he got out alive, he'd go on a tour round South America and when he got back, he'd spend his time planting bombs in barracks.

"Listen," asked the *Santiagueño*, as he shovelled away. "You're the brainy one – how do you say 'I surrender' in English?"

"What, you're already thinking of surrendering?"

"I reckon you don't know."

"You don't have to say anything, all the English need to do is take one look at us and they'll work out for themselves that we're surrendering."

He thought for a while and started up again with questions. "You know what?" he said, pointing to a squat lieutenant, wrapped up in a windproof jacket that every soldier envied. "I'd like to know what the English do with their prisoners."

"I haven't a clue. Ask Molina – his grandma's Irish."

"Hey, Molina," shouted the *Santiagueño*, "what do the English do with their prisoners?"

"I reckon they keep them in the fridge, then make them into

meatballs." Molina was always a great one for tall stories.

"Come off it, I'm serious."

"If they take us," I added just for a bit of drama, "I reckon they'll shoot us all and leave us here on the islands."

"Rubbish," said Oviedo. "The British are incredible ... I knew a Welshman who bred chinchillas. He gave them whisky to drink, poor creatures. You think they'll give us whisky too?"

"Have you read Kipling?"

"I've read Stevenson."

"Stevenson wasn't English."

"So what? The Gurkhas aren't English either, but if they get you, they'll make sure you know who the English are."

"Just think, this lot are leaving behind their summer to die of cold in these islands."

"You know what I say? If they take us prisoner, I reckon they'll make us work like hell. They'll make us build roads, they'll set up building sites, they'll bring water, electricity and we'll end up working till we drop," said the *Santiagueño*.

"Work, here? Listen to this, Viterbo," and Molina called across to Viterbo who was just arriving with half a cigarette in his mouth. "The *Santiagueño* says that if they take us, the English will make us work."

"Why, you're allergic to it?"

"I just don't feel like it, that's all."

"Nor me," said Viterbo. "I've come to fight a war, I'm no builder."

"And I'm a shepherd, I've nothing to do with builders," continued the *Santiagueño*. He came from an Armenian family who worked as shepherds. His grandfather had arrived in the 1930s and had gone to live up in Santiago del Estero. And he, like his grandfather, was a shepherd. He said it was nice living with sheep, that the sheep were happy to let you stroke them at night, and he liked stroking them and being surrounded by sheep.

Five of us were shovelling soil and putting up wooden beams to reinforce the trenches. Time was passing slowly – certain days seemed like an eternity. All of a sudden, Sea Harriers appeared from the clouds, followed by a couple of black specks from anti-aircraft artillery. Missiles dropped from their wings, then we heard a blast, and the earth shook beneath our feet. The planes rose vertically, climbing straight into the clouds and disappeared, leaving a tiny hole in the sky. Far away, at the point where the missiles fell, you could see a mushroom of coloured fire; at first it looked like an orange mushroom, then it turned blue and finally as black as night. The smoke dispersed, carried away by the wind, and we carried on shovelling soil. Every day the same story.

"What could you do with now, most of all?" someone asked, just like that, to break the silence, while he was cleaning his bazooka yet again.

"Me, a good fuck."

"And you?"

"I could do with a large steak, cooked rare, but at this very moment I'd be happy with a bowl of soup," replied the one with the bazooka.

"I want to be on a beach in Bahía, doing what Brazilians do with those Brazilian girls," said another as he watched the manic precision with which his comrade was cleaning his bazooka.

"Me too! And then to roll about in the sand," said another.

"All I want is to sleep for a whole month without waking up."

"You know what I want? To piss in Galtieri's wine glass."

The only one who kept quiet was the *Santiagueño*.

"And you, Santiago del Estero, what would you want, now? To fuck a sheep?"

"No! I want to finish these bloody holes and to get myself inside ... at least I'll have dug myself a grave."

Chapter Seven

About how Corporal Major Cáceres manages to hit an English plane bang on and when I volunteer to go and mine the beaches of Borbón island

In the beginning, the British planes bombed only from a certain height. They had suffered many losses in low-level flying and realized they couldn't underestimate the ramshackle but ferocious Argentine artillery. But Corporal Major Cáceres, a cold, calculating type who spent his time studying every corner of the sky, said he would get them all the same.

"If I've got them in my sight," he said, "those bastards won't get away from me."

Cáceres was one of those people who always had an axe to grind. The face of a scrum-half, stocky build, dark eyes and fiercely patriotic. He was destined for the army right from birth. No one could imagine him without a machine gun in his hands. Ambitious, never satisfied with what fortune brought him and always upset about what it hadn't brought him. During the war, one day at the end of May, he managed to give the best of himself a few kilometres from Puerto Argentino while we were waiting for the English to invade. It was just turning dark, and the wind blew from all directions over that bleak, inhospitable landscape, covered everywhere by a rough grass that not even the wind, which swept it continually, could ever flatten.

That day, as expected, two Harriers appeared high up, seeming at first to be two almost imperceptible holes in the sky. Suddenly one of them veered towards us, trespassing across that barrier which until a few days earlier had kept them well away from our artillery.

"It's breaking away! It's breaking away!" shouted a soldier who had lifted his gun to get it in his sight.

In fact, the plane had broken away and, in a few seconds, began to grow larger before our very eyes. At that moment we rushed into our trench. We had neither the courage nor the equipment to become a band of brave soldiers standing firm in the face of danger, and we disappeared like worms into their holes. And while some retreated and summoned up their last reserves of adrenalin, others went crazy with that hail of gunfire over their heads. On that day in May, the corporal major was the only one with the clearness of mind and readiness to stay there behind his machine-gun. He centred the aircraft in his sights and then began yelling and shooting like a madman. The first volley just managed to graze one side of the plane. He needed to be more accurate, that was clear. The Harrier, having felt the first volley, soared up to join the other plane, but the corporal major's second volley caught it full on. A bull's-eye. At that point the plane dropped four bombs in order, I imagine, to make a quick return without a load. Two exploded close to us and the other two didn't go off; then it rose, leaving a trail of smoke behind it, and disappeared behind the clouds but suddenly reappeared, plummeting like a corkscrew. When it hit the sea, a great scorching bubble shot up from where it fell. At that point, all of us yelled out and went jubilantly to shake hands with the corporal major. He looked at us with that mad, obsessive gaze. "I told you", he said proudly. "Once they're in my sights those bastards won't get away from me. No way!"

There was no doubt about it, this Malvinas machine-gunner was sharp-eyed and had an impeccable style that augured well for the future. Perhaps that was why he treated someone who had no great patriotic pride, like me, with a certain scorn. It's understandable – if you have war in your blood, everything seethes inside you whenever there's mention of an Englishman. But if you haven't, you can't wait to get home and forget all about it. In any event, to stop Cáceres thinking I was an ordinary wimp, I volunteered one day to go and mine the beaches of Borbón Island, north of Gran Malvina. They had assembled us very early one May morning to say they needed two volunteers to go by helicopter, along with Lieutenant Lacarrieu and three other NCOs. I didn't know where Borbón was, but I certainly didn't mind the idea of flying over the Malvinas in a helicopter.

"I'll go, Corporal Major! If I've got to die, I'd be better off doing it away from this lot." The corporal major liked these brave words – and after all, what's the difference between dying in the air or on the ground?

The other soldier who offered to go was Sabelli, a quiet guy with a bull-like neck and protruding chin. He worked as a milkman in civilian life and had no worry about getting up early in the morning. I was never bored with Sabelli, even though he had little to say. He was good company. He had the air of a loner, one of those who seemed detached from everything. I certainly knew Black Pelé better but preferred hanging out with Sabelli. I couldn't have kept up with Pelé – if Pelé had planted thirty mines, I wouldn't have managed more than fifteen or twenty at the most. With Sabelli, on the other hand, I felt on equal terms, for even though he was strong, well built, he was awkward and rather clumsy. So on that May morning, after loading the boxes of anti-personnel mines into the helicopter, we set off for Borbón island. After a few judders, the helicopter blades began to turn, and the bushes were all flattened. It was a large beast with two rotors, one in front and one behind, that shot great pungent blasts of dust and dirt all around it. A ring of damp cold wind had been created, and only at the centre did calm seem to return. Sabelli was sitting down and now looked ahead without saying a word. Like me, he had never travelled in a helicopter. We were behind the three NCOs, our hands propped on the barrels of our guns and our helmets level with our eyebrows. A moment later, we had left the ground and were heading towards the island of Borbón. I felt my stomach drop as I saw everything from up there. The outlines were distinct, but the light had lost all its brilliance. On the sea, however, there was a soft mantle of mist that covered the whole horizon. I'm not quite sure how long it took to get there. After a vertical descent that almost made me puke, the blades brought us to rest on an arid landscape, covered by a thin dark grass, close to the sea. We hurried off at the command of our superiors.

The mines were small, and our work involved digging holes of the same size and putting the mines into them with their heads only just visible: one next to the other. And that was how we planted them, walking backward so as not to tread on them. They were made to explode under the feet of anyone who trod on them. Anything of more than thirty kilos or so, that stood on the exposed head of the mine, would be blown up. Penguins were not at risk, unless they clambered one on top of another and threw themselves down onto them. The ground was boggy, with a few bushes sprouting here and there; I couldn't feel my hands for the cold. I had never planted anything in my life and now I found myself burying those deadly carrots. Christ, when I think of that day! They told me there was a colony of Scottish shepherds living at the centre of the island.

"Strange that someone decides to come and live in the middle of this island, no? And then one day – just think! – once you've settled in nicely, two soldiers like us come along with three NCOs and a lieutenant to plant anti-personnel mines. What do you reckon?" I asked Sabelli, who was five metres away, all silent and wrapped up in his work. He didn't answer, just shrugged his shoulders, which was hardly noticeable, given his stocky build.

That day we planted hundreds of mines. It is said they are still buried there and if anyone wants to go to the island of Borbón – or Pebble Island as the *Kelpers*, the British islanders, call it – they can still see them. Just so long as they don't step on them.

Chapter Eight

About when, holed up in our trenches, we wait for the enemy to arrive and how Atahualpa Yupanqui's *El canto de la tierra* becomes everyone's dream

Before the bombing started, there were days when life, all in all, went by slowly and peacefully. Endless nights and very short days. There was a certain anxious expectation but otherwise everything went on as planned. We were camped there, lost, clueless, our hands frozen, digging enormous holes in the mountains, propping up wooden beams we had to pick up from a naval dockyard. There was snow, but not the sort that comes down in flakes, the kind that falls reluctantly and then covers everything in white. The snow down there was watery and didn't drop vertically but horizontally, driven by the wind, clinging to everything, swirling in the mud, soaking into your clothes. Your helmet was a torture to wear. Marshal Revelio warned us on our very first day, "Your helmet serves not only to protect you from bullets, but also to collect water and, in cases of extreme need, to crap into." No one then could understand what the marshal was talking about, since no soldier imagined we'd have to spend so many days holed up in trenches – and the risk of being caught by the English with your pants down was a risk not even Black Pelé would have run. There was always a shortage of cigarettes, but every so often someone would light one he'd found somewhere and would pass it round his comrades.

"Listen to this," said a soldier who had appeared out of the dark with a crumpled piece of paper in his hands. "The British forces left on 5th April and are arriving here with two aircraft carriers, the *Hermes* and the *Invincible*... three cruisers ... twenty frigates ... two amphibious landing craft ... four nuclear submarines ... forty fighter bombers ... fifty-two combat helicopters ... "

"You're kidding!"

" ... torpedo launchers, rapid-fire guns, anti-ship missiles, anti-missile missiles ..."

"Shit, they mean business."

"... there are thirty warships in all, a forty-five-thousand-ton transatlantic liner ... In short, these English ... get the picture?"

The soldier put the piece of paper into his pocket and passed the cigarette he had in his mouth, which was now almost out, to someone who was leaning for a moment on the handle of his shovel.

"Then they've got it into their heads to win?"

"And the Russians, when are the Russians arriving?" someone else asked, leaning across to take the cigarette butt which was almost finished.

"Yes, the Russians ..."

"And the Peruvians, weren't the Peruvians going to give us a hand?"

"Perhaps you haven't understood ... this is a war against the English, backed by the Americans ... what have the Peruvians got to do with it?"

"Look at the Incas, they used to be ..."

"This lot have massive submarines, one machine-gun per person, thermal suits, and you're telling me about the Incas!"

"Who cares about submarines if we're here on land?"

"Mine the fields ... then we'll see if they have the courage to pass through them."

"And the helicopters?"

"And food, there's nothing to eat on these islands?"

"If they carry on giving us *maté cocido* tea and freeze-dried rations, they won't need many bombs to finish us off."

"You have no faith – we're writing the history of our country here!"

Then there were the first rumbles of artillery, cooking pans scraped to the bottom, and the wind that never stopped blowing. Every so often I would read a poem from *El grito de la langosta* which, according to Carlitos, ought to prevent Surrealism from getting stuck in its oneiric rut. But there was never a chance of reading in peace down there. Each time, sooner or later, you'd get called by an NCO who ordered you to clean something or reinforce a trench. "Put some beams in my trench as well, just like the captain's."

Then we'd take a piece of sheet metal, two strong beams, dig down deeper, and once we had finished would return to our shelters. Obedience and precision, two qualities drummed into us from the very first day. But was it worth it, I wondered, being stuck there in those hideouts with no option but to wait for the enemy to arrive? And did this presumed enemy know we were hidden there in those camouflaged dens among bushes and rocks? And what were we supposed to do when they arrived? Jump up and shoot like mad? And then? And there again, I wondered, how would the enemy react to our very predictable plan? And those mines down there by the beach? It wouldn't be so difficult to put together those three or four synapses necessary to reach the conclusion that hidden in that forbidding landscape was a patrol just waiting for them to arrive. We weren't dealing with amateurs. Everyone knows that the English have been fighting wars since time immemorial. And they must have known perfectly well we were down there, ready to defend our cause. The rainwater streamed into our trenches, and to get it out was no easy task. In the end, our helmets came in useful even for this. Carlitos was right: *The world is nothing but misery and frustration*, as he wrote in a line very much in vogue among the regulars at Tío Pablo's. And what would happen if all of us – Argentines, English, Gurkhas or whoever – stopped helping the war machine that had been set into motion? Is it possible, I wondered, to reject war when thousands of people gather in a public square and cheer the armed invasion and ask you to take up a gun to defend the Malvinas, which have always *llevan en el corazón*? It was our misfortune to have to get them back. "*Las Malvinas son nuestras*," Lieutenant Owen would say in bold defiance, "*argentinas desde siempre*". Now it was for us to go and claim them back, thirty poor wretches hiding away in those holes full of water.

"Hey, Alberto, what are you thinking about?" asked the *Santiagueño*, stuck there in the hole next to mine and frightened like me.

"I'm not thinking anything, *Santiagueño*," I said. "I'm cold and there's water coming in everywhere."

"The water's coming in here too, brother," he said in that sing-song voice.

"Silence!" This voice was clipped, guttural, sounding as if two or three voices had been put together to say the same thing. "Keep alert. You understand?"

"Yes, lieutenant," said the *Santiagueño* before falling silent.

The enemy could appear at any moment. And we carried on fingering the beads of our rosaries, repeating the same old prayer, throwing the water out with our helmets.

I remember the strange feeling I had when I read the newspapers, which always arrived late: *The Malvinas in Argentine hands ... Reagan: "I never imagined the Argentines would invade the islands" ... The English assemble the greatest fleet since the end of World War Two ... Task Force mobilized ... Argentina responds ...* The newspapers often showed a photo taken by someone called Wallman of the English surrender on April 2: four English marines with their hands up and an Argentine officer pointing something out to them. And then I thought of those war films where you saw soldiers shot dead with their hands up.

Each of us had to eat and sleep as best we could, living on our wits. The important thing was not to get caught *in flagrante*, otherwise you'd get the *estaqueo*, which involved being staked to the ground with your arms wide apart and left out all night in the bitter cold. One night of *estaqueo* was enough to drive you mad.

During the action, everyone was frightened of crossing the field to get to the hospital infirmary. It was a hard job getting there. And then, inside that place overflowing with half-drugged casualties was enough to make you throw up. At first, we carried away the dead. As time passed the bodies were left where they fell. Every so often you heard an aircraft showering bombs. The air turned black, with an acid that made your eyes burn for hours. You'd feel the explosion inside you even after a couple of days (if you were lucky enough still to feel it). The dead were dead, and you couldn't risk your own life taking them to the infirmary. But the wounded were taken there, since there is still life in the wounded, as Captain Correas used to remind us. If there was a Jeep, they'd be carried by Jeep or in the Unimog, otherwise they'd be put on a stretcher and carried through the firing line on foot. Argentine planes landed close to the infirmary, flying in reinforcements, flying out the wounded, as well as bringing supplies of medicine and food for the officers. The war would have carried on unhindered so long as the planes could supply the base. Captain Correas, on one of those trips, managed to get hold of a small stereo with a dozen cassette tapes and one evening he let us hear *El canto de la tierra* by Atahualpa Yupanqui. It was strange that he let us hear Atahualpa Yupanqui, whom the military rulers had targeted for years. *El canto de la tierra* remained inside me after that evening, and I heard it in silence over the days to come, hiding away in my trench, while the English machine-guns fired away beyond the mountains. I imagined that other soldiers might also be listening to *El canto de la tierra* in their trenches and that, maybe, now and then, they were sticking out their guns and firing two or three random shots so that the English could see they were responding to their offensive. But by now the soldiers weren't there any longer, getting pulped in the mud, because at that moment they were on the vast plains of the Pampas walking quietly along solitary paths, listening to the guitar of Atahualpa Yupanqui, or resting under the shade of a tree. Then Captain Correas would bark at us in that abrupt manner of his. "Where are you firing, you idiots? The English are across there, keep your eyes open!" He'd say this though he didn't know what on earth was going on. By now I was imagining that the whole troop was part of *El canto de la tierra* and it was only by chance that we happened to be there fighting a war in the Malvinas, on those mountains, when in fact we were in the Pampas. I'd have been happy if Captain Correas was with us under the sun of those vast plains, with the voice of Atahualpa Yupanqui reaching us from the four corners of the horizon, rather than being here always giving orders like a lunatic, trying to find the best way of bumping off as many Englishmen as possible.

It was more or less like this: when the Sea Harriers were about to arrive, the air around us changed completely. You could hear something far off, a humming that came from the sea, the clouds dropped down and we gave the alert.

"Attention, attention, alarm!"

Atahualpa Yupanqui's voice at that moment became darker, overwhelmed by the sound of the planes. Then, when the Sea Harriers went back into the clouds, his voice returned as luxuriant as before to sing out the feelings of the earth. But it was followed straightaway by another resounding boom, more powerful than the one before. You felt it in you, the muscles of your body came away from the bones, and your spirit left your body for an instant, or forever. Your spirit was watching you from far away, hanging from a white parachute that dropped down slowly. "Hey Alberto!" it said, and you could hear yelling, confusion everywhere, bullets hammering into the ground, the mournful voice of Atahualpa

Yupanqui between the chords of a guitar, orders you couldn't understand, then an explosion and another one, and the ground would shake under your feet. Smoke mushroomed as high as apartment blocks. Someone was saying the Lord's Prayer, another was cursing into the wind or repeating multiplication tables, everything was transformed into a raging inferno. Soldiers were going here and there, shouting out to each other, others were running about as never before or staring at the sky with eyes wide open.

"What's happening, Alberto?" my spirit asked.

"Hell, I haven't a clue what's going on," my body replied, "all I know is that I was listening quietly to *El canto de la tierra* and now I'm dying like a starved rat."

"Hey Alberto!" said my spirit once again. "Do something, for God's sake!"

"We're coming back," the English seemed to be telling us. "You ought to be far too scared to sleep, far too scared to eat ... even if you have nothing to eat. We're going to make you wait."

When the British planes had gone back to their aircraft carriers, the spirit returned and attached itself to the body once more, or sometimes it went away forever. Then, all fell into deep silence. We got out of our trenches and *El canto de la tierra* once again echoed in the south wind. The clouds returned to where they had been and a black blanket of smoke rose, clogging our lungs. Finally, the cries of the wounded started up, and of those tending them.

The first death I saw was Zukovskij's. We called him *el rusito*, the little Russian. He wasn't Catholic and yet he wore a tremendous crucifix. Somebody in the troop had given it to him, urging him never to take it off. When I found him, he was lying on the ground with his arms stretched out and a great piece of shrapnel stuck in his stomach. That was how he went, in that undignified way, amid the shouts of soldiers and machine-gun fire. He had just turned nineteen and was lying there in the mud, his clothes soaked in blood, and everyone was calling for help, though on that day not even God Almighty could have saved Zukovskij *el rusito*.

I first met *el rusito* while we were transporting a twelve-metre gun that had arrived from Comodoro Rivadavia airport. I heard him talk for the first time. He stammered like a spluttering engine. When he got stuck, those he was talking to quietly waited. But sometimes it took him so long to say things that someone would start laughing or slap him on the back.

And we were yelling, "*Rusito, Rusito!*" And there was blood gushing everywhere. We had to take him to the infirmary by stretcher and ask for reinforcements straightaway. "Reinforcements? For what?" I wondered. What we really needed was a white flag to wave at those fucking English. Another nineteen-year-old was arriving to take his place, a boy with acne, scared and as skinny as a rake; around his neck he wore an aluminium medal with his name inscribed, so that they knew who to send condolences to if the need arose. They'd packed him up and sent him to the front line, and now he found himself plunked in a hole, his face wild with panic. "You stay here and when the bombs arrive, run or shoot your gun, do as you like, we're at war and there's no time to lose."

"Yes, sir!" replied the nineteen-year-old.

And I wanted to go back to *El canto de la tierra*, to hold my girlfriend close in my arms and tell my grandpa that in this war, damn it, they were throwing all they could at us, these English ... to hell with all of them. Why were they bombing us like this? For a few windswept islands? They could keep their islands! And fuck it, why kill people like this, for a few islands?

Chapter Nine

About the drunken antics of my friends, myself included, and how one evening, through the fault of the great poet of the hangover (Carlitos), we run off for fear of being beaten up by a huge man weighing a ton and a half

After my return from the Malvinas, I was someone who, by and large, drank regularly but carefully. I subjected my liver to continuous exertion, though without pushing it too far. And when, as occasionally happened, I felt the world spinning around, I found some excuse to leave Tío Pablo's and wander the city streets. Irlandés was also someone who drank regularly, but much more than me. By the afternoon, he had settled himself at his usual table, rolled up his sleeves and began drinking beer. "My alcohol-free afternoon," he used to call it. After that he drank whisky or vodka until late evening. He was the first to arrive at Tío Pablo's and the last to go. Sitting there, Irlandés was a quiet sort: he drank, reading the newspaper or a book. He was quiet for hours, then all at once he'd start reminiscing and laughing to himself. While he was sitting down, he held his alcohol very well, though he drank hard, but the problem was when he decided to stand up. At that moment his whole great drunkenness went to his head, and he could hold it no longer. This was the secret behind his immobility. Carlitos, on the other hand, drank every so often and preferred smoking joints, but when he got drunk he did so in such a way that he had to remain shut up at home for several days to recover. And that was when he wrote his poetry. He started on *El grito de la langosta* at a time when alcohol had put him entirely out of action. "Here we are again ... the great poet of the hangover," Irlandés would say when he re-emerged with a bundle of poems under his arm.

"What can I do about it? It's my weakness, writing sobers me up!" he used to say.

Among our circle of friends, he was known as the poet-of-the-day-after. None of the regulars at Tío Pablo's cared much for his poetry, and if I'm honest nor did I, but Carlitos was nevertheless regarded as someone destined for great things. He was always generous towards those who liked to call themselves poets because, after all, he was better than all of them, even though he was a poet inundated by letters of refusal, and would still have been, even if he hadn't written another line of poetry.

Everyone at Tío Pablo's drank – some more than others – and everyone pretended they were on the point of leaving, especially when they were out of money and thirsty. "I'm getting out of this country, I'm going tomorrow ... that's right, I'm going to Brazil and never coming back."

No one ever asked, for example, "But what are you going to do in Brazil?" Or, "Try doing some work, perhaps you could earn a few pesos." There was a tacit understanding among drinkers: if there was no money to be spent on drink, you might just as well go off to Brazil and live in a shack by the sea.

Here, like the outskirts of all large cities, there was no shortage of "velvet rottweilers", those who arrive late and gather one or two people around them to propose some scheme that cannot fail: a bank, a consignment of marijuana, a little money on the side. Those involved in that kind of dealing were at the table at the far end, under the portrait of Carlos Gardel. And those who went to Tío Pablo's and wanted nothing to do with the rottweilers avoided the far end.

We would generally stay there until the usual police car arrived and the same cop signalled from the window that it was time to close. The barman would point to the customers still at the bar and go to the window saying, "How can I get rid of them? They're still drinking!"

"I don't care, just get rid of them and close up," the cop would say, and leave straightaway, without another word.

"Okay guys," the barman would say in a tone of melancholy. "You've heard. The authorities say you have to leave."

It was obvious that Irlandés and the rottweilers at the far end would start protesting and cursing the police, the military, and every city authority. But some remained behind the closed shutters for another half hour while the barman finished mopping the floor; others went off to the station bar which was always open, day and night.

The hardest time of the day was when you had to find the courage to return home.

One evening, after the usual cop had ordered the place to close, Carlitos, Irlandés and I went to a bar near San Miguel hospital which, for some reason or other, could remain open till morning. We sat down at a table and gave our order.

"A whisky for me," said Irlandés.

"And for me," I said.

"Two whiskies for the gentlemen, and for you?" said the barman to Carlitos.

"I'd like a vodka."

"Sorry, we've finished the vodka."

"How come? You have everything, but no vodka?"

"That's right, I'm afraid we don't."

"That's strange."

"Well, I'm sorry, but it's not so unusual. We've got no vodka. That's all there is to it."

"I've never seen a bar without vodka."

"Then it's the first time," said the barman, looking across to the bar.

It seemed strange to me too that they had no vodka, but I didn't want to let Carlitos know, otherwise he'd use it as an excuse to begin yet another argument. In this respect I admired him. He would never stoop to drinking anything other than what his taste required. In such a situation, Irlandés would have taken something else if there was no vodka, but not Carlitos, the poet-of-the-day-after, who in such matters was very choosy.

"So then, have you decided?" the barman asked again.

"I'll have a vodka."

"Well, you're a fine sort, eh?" snorted the barman, raising his eyebrows. "I tell you for the last time: there's no vodka. That's it."

"Tell me then as soon as it arrives."

The barman glowered at him and left.

Two women in miniskirts were talking at the bar with a customer, one of those pimps who deal in the impossible, who take two or three grams each evening and surround themselves with women who are just as stoned as they are.

"Here are your whiskies," said the barman as he returned.

"I've asked for a vodka," insisted Carlitos.

"OK, first pay for the two whiskies," said the barman, turning to him, though he'd still had nothing to drink.

"No, first bring me what I've ordered and then we'll pay for everything together."

He hadn't even finished the sentence when a man appeared, weighing about a ton and a half, a shabby replica of that pimp who was talking to the women. He stopped at the table with the idea of sorting them out.

"Who's the smart-ass who wants the vodka?" he asked in a Pantagruelian tone, as he wiped a layer of nicotine from his grimy moustache and sniffed up the last traces of coke.

"I'm the one who wants it, why?" said Carlitos, getting to his feet. I was stunned by his defiance. That the poet-of-the-day-after, so thin and puny, should think of taking on that Samson from the Buenos Aires underworld was an act of unimaginable folly. This was the kind of person who ought to have gone fighting down in the Malvinas to lose a bit of flab, I thought.

"Ah, it's you?" And while the brute was about to give him a right hook, Carlitos managed to get in first with a fairly effective blow to the stomach. It wasn't his style to sort out arguments with a punch-up, but this time we were all up for it. How ill-advised it was to respond to such threats. That punch had no effect, but it gave us enough time to scarper as fast as we could. The barman chased us for a short distance but turned round and could see no sign of the brute, so went back.

"Next time you won't know what's hit you," shouted the barman from far off.

"And all this for a vodka!" I observed.

"Which they didn't even have," added Irlandés.

"Let's go and get a beer at the station," said Carlitos at last, lifting his middle finger at the barman. "This area's full of morons."

Chapter Ten

Which tells of my aunt Albertina who's no longer right in the head and the day Francisca takes me to her spiritual guide to free me from the evil eye

Things had taken a nasty turn for the worse. My grandpa had died on 16th June, at the end of the war, my girlfriend no longer wanted to make love with me, and my aunt Albertina, grandpa Pasquale's sister, had started to lose her marbles. Aunt Albertina hadn't been right in the head for some time, but by the second half of 1982 it seemed as though someone had got inside her brain and was jumbling up her thoughts. She wouldn't leave the house. She spent the whole day watching people walking along the street. My mother sat her by the front door, and she stayed there till evening. She took a final turn for the worse after her brother's death, and now her memory had gone off on its own sweet way. She could no longer connect anything together. She used to get confused over family relationships, she wanted to say one thing and ended up saying another, like the time she wanted to be taken to the toilet but said she wanted the pasta instead, and then pissed herself and everyone told her off. And yet we understood each other quite well: I told her things, even things about the war, and she nodded yes with her head and smiled, showing those three or four remaining teeth. I liked to sit drinking *maté* with her, while people said hello to her from the street: "Good morning, *doña* Albertina."

"Good morning," she'd reply, and she would carry on watching until the passer-by had disappeared.

"Don't let her drink too much – she'll only wet herself and get high blood pressure," my mother would say, but I secretly gave her a little extra *maté* all the same. She used to close her mouth and suck through pursed lips.

I always called Aunt Albertina "auntie". I believe I inherited my name from her.

"Aunt Albertina," I asked, "did you ever have any boyfriends?"

My aunt nodded and smiled, covering her hand, pleased that I was interested in her love life.

"And what were these boyfriends like, auntie?" She shrugged her shoulders and carried on smiling, pushing her tongue through the gap between some missing teeth.

She once told me that a certain Giovanni Pupputuro, known as the Count, had once greeted her from the saddle of his horse while she was walking home along a lane, and she had been so captivated by that great centaur that, when she told me, it seemed as though she was revealing some deep secret. She remembered Giovanni Pupputuro and his nag very well, and that day she told me all about him – this was before she started going mad and before I went off into the army. She took me to her bedroom, opened the wardrobe which she called her dresser, took out a box and showed me a letter he had sent her from Italy. I took hold of the letter, which was edged with the colours of the Italian flag, turned it round, then checked the address. The postmark was from Campobasso and it had been sent in October 1953.

"But auntie," I said after a pause, "this letter is sealed."

She stared at me with a look of resignation. Then she smiled. "Of course, I have never opened it."

"Never opened it, but why, Auntie?"

"Because that's how it is." She held the letter to her chest without saying another word.

From that day on, Aunt Albertina had become someone to whom I knew I could say anything, or almost anything.

*

… and in one of those long hot Buenos Aires afternoons, I told her my world had split in two in 1982 when Francisca, my then girlfriend, had met her spiritual guide, a sorceress who had snatched her from my arms to introduce her to who-knows-what mysterious truth. From that moment our relationship fell to pieces. She had stopped drinking and singing with me, she came to Tío Pablo's only to preach at me. Then she would go home and shut herself in her room to meditate.

And yet, when I was down there, with the wind numbing my bones, I found solace in writing letters in which I told her, if I survived the war, that we would never leave each other ever again.

When you're cold, hungry, and tired, and the enemy's lobbing missiles at you from the other side of the mountain, and you're stuck in these trenches with your back in pieces, covered in mud, waiting for something to take you far away from it all, well, my darling Francisca, at a moment like this, writing a letter is the last remaining hope. Two months have passed, and I still have no news from you; to be honest, my comrades haven't received any letters either, which makes me think they've all been lost, thrown into the sea like dead things. It doesn't matter. I feel you close to me all the same, and I hold you tight, like this lousy gun.

Instead, when I got back from down there with my head still full of the war, my girlfriend used to spend all the time talking about the hereafter and positive energy.

"What's all this positive energy, Francisca?" I asked. She explained that positive energy is something that surrounds you like a light and makes you see the world from high above.

"From high above where?"

"From high above in the heavens," she said.

"The only things high above in the heavens are fighter-bombers."

"You know, auntie, I've never been much of a believer or superstitious," I told my aunt Albertina when I talked to her about these things that neither I, nor she, could understand. "I can't be bothered, auntie, about touching my balls each time a black cat crosses the road. I ended up being bribed to go to catechism, remember? And I've never lit a candle for anyone, not even for the poor soul of your brother, God bless him, so I'm hardly going to feel surrounded by a light. Nor have I ever felt touched by the wings of the hereafter. And yet I find myself there with Francisca who's telling me about the hereafter and positive energy."

My auntie didn't know whether to smile or look serious. "I told you, didn't I, oranges go bad in this heat?" she said, patting my knee with her hand.

I told Aunt Albertina about things that happened before I went into the army, when Francisca and I used to go to Tío Pablo's for our drink together, and I kept the situation under control. My poor auntie often clapped her hands ... I know she didn't understand what I was saying, but she tried as best she could.

"We loved each other, auntie. I liked seeing Francisca half drunk," I said, "and always willing. We used to sing on the terrace at her place. Her breath would smell of cheap whisky and I kissed her, and our tongues wrapped together, and the Malvinas weren't there, auntie, nor the English, nor that dickhead Sergeant Alcalde, and I kept the situation under control, and life was there in Francisca's breath that smelt of cheap whisky. I was eighteen, auntie, and I had a hard-on all the time, and she was seventeen and always wet, and we could get drunk whenever we wanted because we were happy singing on the terrace at her place and not being swallowed up by the war," I told my auntie.

*

…but I couldn't work out, after I got back, why Francisca wanted to take me to the house of her spiritual guide, and why that woman, who was helping her to find her way through the labyrinth of the soul, was so anxious to meet me.

"But Francisca, can't you understand?" I said. "The English almost killed me and now you want to take me to your spiritual guide. I don't even know what a spiritual guide is! The lads were dying and there were certainly no spiritual guides to see us down there."

"She'll help you. She'll help you sort yourself out," Francisca told me. "She's a woman who understands everything from the energy you give out."

This woman had told Francisca, among other things, that some jinx had put an evil eye on me, out of envy or for some other reason, and it had to be taken away, otherwise the evil eye would, in some mysterious way, affect the process of reaching her soul.

"And what have I got to do with all this?"

"All she has to do is look into your eyes."

"I've got nothing in my eyes, I'm perfectly okay."

"That's what you think."

"So far as I'm concerned, what I think is good enough for me."

"But maybe you're not the only one in the world."

"And so?"

"So you need to come along."

Once she had an idea in her head, there was no way of getting rid of it.

"Alright then," I said in the end, "let's get rid of this evil eye and then we can forget all about it, but you've got to understand I'm doing it for you, because this evil eye is no bother to me; as a matter of fact, if some Englishman has put it there, I'd rather like to keep it as a souvenir."

*

72

Francisca's spiritual guide lived in the Manuelita district, a suburb of squat houses and dirt roads. You get there across a small stream of filthy water where the inhabitants throw all their rubbish. We were welcomed on our arrival by barking dogs and people at their doorways who said nothing but looked at us suspiciously. The house of the spiritual guide was yet another example of South American baroque paganism: saints, statues, lighted candles, three thousand Christs, a smiling Evita, a portrait of Ceferino Namuncurá, a gilt, carved cross, a small flag with the image of a bearded saint. There was also a small altar with vases full of chrysanthemums and two red velvet cushions on it. The soothsayer's family were a bunch of wretches: one son in prison, a daughter pregnant, another who was running around barefoot chasing a hen that took shelter behind a rusty galvanized iron shack, a drunkard husband who stole the offerings made by jinxed renegades like me ... she was a short round woman, an artificial blonde with black hair regrowing from the roots: she preached eternal love and reconciliation with the Lord. She had been a sad, mistreated child who'd arrived from the darkest Middle Ages to become a modern-day witch. When we entered the house, she sat us down on a bright blue sofa and then, with the calm that such a ritual required, poured holy water onto her hands. With her purified hands, she took mine and led me in silence to the window overlooking the chicken house. I did what she said, I didn't want to go against her or ask questions. I stood there, still, in front of the window. She stared strangely at me, though she didn't frighten me. I assumed this stare was the prelude to some state of trance or visit to her guardian spirits. She went into another room and came back with a shiny pair of scissors and a basin of hot coals. As she placed it all on the windowsill, I looked anxiously at Francisca. "What do I have to do now?" I wondered.

"Don't worry, she uses them to ward off evil spirits," said Francisca with a friendly smile, referring to the scissors.

"You have to keep still," added the spiritual guide.

"Does it hurt?" I asked quietly, though I had resolved not to ask questions.

The sorceress answered with the look of her eye and came closer. I could feel her odour more strongly, a blend of citric acid and hamburger which mingled with the smoke from the basin. She asked me to close my eyes, but as I hadn't understood, she touched my arm with a finger, saying, "I said, you have to close your eyes." I apologized with a hand gesture and closed them reluctantly.

I wasn't at all happy about the whole business, not least because I had no idea what the hell she was about to do with the scissors. I obeyed all the same, and stood there motionless, waiting. The sorceress started scissoring around me, as if she were playing about, not touching me, but just to annoy me. She was scissoring around my head, my arms, my legs; perhaps she wanted to cut me away from the rest of the room, an idea that I didn't mind one little bit because at that very moment all I wanted was to get out of that place, never to return. Meanwhile she was muttering under her breath – a prayer in Guaraní, an invocation to the saints. Then she started talking more loudly, with a voice that didn't sound like hers. "Away with you! Leave this Christian alone! Get out and never come back!" And meanwhile she carried on scissoring madly around me, as if she were fighting some imaginary swordsman.

After ten minutes or so she suddenly stopped, raised my eyelids with her fingers and peered into my pupils. I don't know what she saw inside but, from the way she looked at me, it seemed as though the whole business of the evil eye had gone badly wrong. I stood there with my eyes open and, turning away with a hand over her mouth, she went towards the window and immediately opened it. Leaning out, she let off such an enormous burp that the hens perching on the steps scuttled off in fright. I wanted to laugh but was so exhausted that I didn't have the energy. I also noticed that Francisca was very serious, and this made me realize we'd reached a delicate moment. Just then, the sorceress filled her lungs once more and gave off another incredible burp without the slightest embarrassment. I let myself drop onto the sofa. I had no idea what the devil she'd been doing with those scissors. I felt lighter, as if she'd removed some invisible monster coiled around my spine; in fact, I now felt as if my spine was suspended in air without the support of my legs. It felt rather like when I smoked my first joints. I could hear talking, but they were just voices, far away, which came into my head as if through a tube. After fifteen minutes or so I got up, by myself, and slowly went back to feeling as I had done before. I felt as if that invisible monster was once again coiled around my spine. I was about to tell the witch that I felt touched by the evil eye just as before, but then I had second thoughts. Perhaps I couldn't have lived without that monster around my spine. In fact, all I wanted to do just then was light a cigarette and get a drink. At Tío Pablo's, I thought, with a story like that, I'd be able to get as drunk as I liked. What I wanted to know was what she had released with those burps: some evil idol that was pushing on my cornea? A chemistry of air and incorporeal beings? I didn't have the courage to ask. But I had to admit it was very kind of her: she had removed the whole of my evil eye without knowing how much money I was going to leave in the offertory basket – or whether I was going to leave anything at all.

"And if the evil eye had decided it wasn't going to leave her body?" I thought as I sat on her bright blue sofa. "If her oesophagus had closed up at that very moment and she hadn't been able to burp?"

Once the whole ceremony was over, she sat beside me. You could see from her eyes that the sucking had left her exhausted. Now, I thought, she began to seem more pleasant. Once she had recovered, she began talking about disentanglement of the soul. *It's a question of balance, you see? That's what it needs. The virile power has to be defused, understand?* She told me, in short, that Francisca was going through a difficult time, and it would be better to observe a certain chastity. *A certain chastity! Just like that. For a war veteran, you understand, that's unthinkable. And then, excuse me, if a merciful God really exists, then there's no way he's going to leave this randy young man just back from the war to suffer like that.* I was about to say that I preferred Francisca as she was before: *and look here, I'm no lecher, I consider myself to be more a sober-minded platonic.* She asked me to help her just the same, and to know that she would one day return Francisca to me with her soul all disentangled.

"With her soul disentangled?" I asked.

"You shall see," she replied.

Chapter Eleven

About when, two years after the war, I leave my city behind, and my father takes me to the airport

I'm walking with a small group of prisoners. There's no Englishman leading us, and perhaps we haven't even been taken prisoner, but we walk in silence, with our feet caked in mud. The planes are destroying the trenches above Moody Brook and the guns of the Seventh regiment have been silenced. "We're a group of sheep rustlers," I think to myself. I open the water-bottle hanging from my belt, I turn it and let the stones inside it fall out. "I surrendo, I surrendo," comes a voice with a strong Argentine accent from the other side of the mountain.

I wake with my heart pounding, go into the kitchen and gulp down some cold water. Then I return to bed, but I can't sleep any more.

The war finished two years ago and yet each time, every night, I still end up on the losing side. As soon as I shut my eyes and silence falls, that's when the trouble starts. And yet, during the daytime I would enjoy remembering those things I dreamed about at night. As time went by, I began thinking that sooner or later I'd have to leave my country. Perhaps somewhere where I could think and speak another language – I felt imprisoned by words here. Everything turned my thoughts to the Malvinas, the trenches, my feet caked in mud, the helicopters. My father would say, "You ought to learn a new language from scratch, so you can think and dream without the memory of those old words. A new language, new freedom." It was the first time I ever told him he was right.

But if I had sorted myself out, then I certainly wouldn't have left my country. I would still have held on to my Castilian, I would have carried on going to the library to read Plotinus, and by evening I'd have closed myself up at Tío Pablo's drinking beer. But for some time now, the city and its memories had been bugging me. The woman at the travel agency who sold me the ticket for Italy had a different point of view. According to her, if you can't sort yourself out here, she said, the best thing to do is go off travelling, take a trip round the world. To some extent I agreed, even though I had always found journeys very tiring. And there again, when you're travelling, you leave and then come back, and all I wanted to do at that time was just get away.

It was my father who took me to Buenos Aires airport on the day of my departure. I was carrying with me twenty years of my life packed into a leather suitcase – a pair of woollen socks, a velvet shirt, a pair of trousers, two undershirts, a book by Felisberto Hernández, another by Ezequiel Martínez Estrada, and Cortázar of course; in other words, those few things that any twenty-year-old of my generation couldn't have managed without. The exercise book that John Smith had given me I left for my sister. "You can have this," I said. "It belonged to an English soldier I met on the *Canberra*."

"And what am I supposed to do with it?"

"Nothing, just look at it once in a while."

Then my father and I looked out of a large window and saw the Boeing ready to take off for Rome, with the sun glinting on the runway. "I could still change my mind," I thought, looking out at that vast causeway which ended up where I would have to start all over again. I felt rather dazed, as Irlandés would say when he got up in the morning, but I knew I was doing something important. Until that moment I didn't believe I would really end up at an airport taking a flight across the ocean, never to return.

"If there's no one there to help you, you've got to do it yourself," I said.

At some point, as I was looking at the plane, I felt my father's heavy hands on my shoulders, and I don't know why I remembered the time when I had returned to Buenos Aires for the first time, on board a four-engine plane that had taken me from the city of Trelew to El Palomar airport. When we got off the plane, they put us onto lorries. It was the middle of the night, and they were taking us to Sargento Cabral school at the Campo de Mayo barracks. Just outside the airport fence was a group of mothers asking for news of their sons. "Danielito, Danielito Diaz... do you know Daniel Diaz?" one of them asked. None of us knew what to say, whether her son Danielito was alive or dead. We had also been told not to talk to anyone and not to give information of any kind. All of us had to remain completely silent. The convoy of lorries was driving along a dark road and the mothers were following us, running along the perimeter fence, desperately crying out the names of their sons. I was thinking that my mother could have been there among those women, or the mother of Zukovskij, *el rusito*. The city was there, extending out towards the river. To one side we could see the grey sleeping mass of apartment blocks and, to the other, mothers who were still calling out for their sons. We watched them from where we were sitting in our lorries, saying not a word, and they were left behind, on the other side of the perimeter fence, without an answer.

A female voice announced the flight for Rome. Then my father looked at me and said, "Write as soon as you can, let us know something."

I gave him a hug and once more felt his large hands on my shoulders. That moment cancelled out all the misunderstandings, all the arguments; I was there in his arms like a little boy, until he looked at me and said, "You remember the time of that accident with the bus, when I got out of the car and was in such a state that I was going to smash up all the windows?"

"Of course I remember."

"And that time when I lost everything, remember?"

"I remember that as well."

"And you remember those fellows who were looking for me and came asking where I was."

"I remember… I was still small then."

"Well, make sure you don't go doing what I did. Okay?"

"I'm twenty, and I promise not to do anything that you did."

"That's what I like to hear. Good luck, look after yourself."

I got onto the escalator that went up to the departure lounge, and he stayed down below watching me. I sat down on a seat thinking that he too, many years before, had waved goodbye to his own family from the rail of a ship. At that moment, thoughts about the existence of some kind of destiny seemed something quite relevant. Fortunately, I had brought a small bottle of whisky with me in a box, and from one swig to the next I began to feel a little stronger. After the sixth or the seventh swig, I felt ready to hand my ticket to the hostess who looked at me with a friendly smile, the typical smile of a hostess who always has a ready welcome. Once I had settled down in my seat, I thought that maybe, from the other side of the world, I might at last succeed in getting that war which had been pestering me for two years out of my head. The plane was about to take off. From the window I could see a long grey highway that disappeared into the distance.

"*Adiós mi querida Buenos Aires* and may God be with you!"

Chapter Twelve

About when in Italy I receive letters from my friend Carlitos and each time I start Malvinizing again and my nightmares come back

And here I am, in a shack looking out over the Adriatic Sea, with my grandpa's chain round my neck. Below me there is a road lined with poplars that takes you to the sea, but before you reach it, you have to go downhill through the last remnants of countryside. From there you cross the overpass and then you suddenly arrive at the beach. There's also another way of reaching the sea, if you want to get there from the group of houses on the ridge, but if you go that way you have to take the dirt road that passes the Latini's house. Those who take the shortcut find that everyone else in this area goes this way. The bulldog at the Latini's house will of course rush to the fence when it hears you walking past and will carry on growling until you've passed the elm tree; Pallotta's white cow will peer curiously at you as though it has never seen another being in that area and you will wonder what it's thinking behind those bovine eyes; then you'll usually come across a couple of old people sitting by the doorway of the last house. Everything seems asleep along this road which passes through the fields, and it has taken me years to realize that's not the case. Every day since I've been living here, I wander through the fields and enjoy finding the crows on the eaves. There are also pheasants, but they are too timid, and they hide among the corn as soon as they hear anyone. But I miss the birds of my own city, those vast flocks that arrive from the delta, flying over the roofs of the apartment blocks. Here I have learned to shovel snow and talk like my grandparents used to do. Fortunately, I can now sleep the whole night without waking up in front of an English firing squad, which is already a great step forward. But when I get letters from Carlitos, postmarked San Miguel, in an envelope with an edging of light blue and white vertical lines and chaotic handwriting, I start Malvinizing again and in the evening my nightmares return.

Dear Alberto,

I've been mucking around for a year now with my book on the war in the Malvinas, Sonata for Voice and Gun. *I write, cross out, rewrite and so on. So far as possible, I try not to miss my meals and to get my ideas clear, but sometimes, when I'm sitting there in front of the typewriter, I feel I have to reach some sort of decision about the points that are plaguing me. It's the idea of the war that keeps me awake at night, that feeling of uselessness in the midst of all those bullets whizzing around you. Do you think the fact I wasn't there in the remote Atlantic, fighting in the cold, in the snow, among the penguins, prevents me from writing about the war? I don't know what it means to find myself behind a gun; I've never spent a single day in a barracks; on my identity card there's a nice red stamp, now faded, which says: Unfit for all Active Duty, and after that, in blue ink, it specifies the type of unfitness. In my case it's mental. So I'm not an ex-soldier. And I've read Céline, Vonnegut and few others on the war. Does this stop me telling the story of a soldier who escapes from the bombings and escapes during the retreat from the front line?*

I also told Irlandés what I wanted to write, and he started laughing, as usual, and had another drink. I can't understand why you still insist on avoiding the whole question, why you don't want to talk about the war. Couldn't you salvage something out of that great defeat of yours? If you just happened to end up on those islands down there, while you were still just a kid, there's no point silently afflicting yourself for so long over it. Nerves are a serious business – if you don't get it out of your system, it makes things

82

worse ... I know from experience. "Well done, soldier Alberto Adorno, co-operate with our de-Malvinization process," you'll receive the thanks of the first duty officer.

And now, you've made this great return to Italy that your family had always wanted to make. And what do you get up to in the evening, apart from going to bed early? Who knows why everyone who leaves here thinks, at first, that the country they have moved to is fantastic, full of wonderful things and they write enthusiastic letters to everyone, but then after a while they begin to get as bored as hell, and become bitter. They start making comparisons: "The people here are like this, but they're better there because they do such-and-such," and so on. And they are convinced their homeland, despite everything, is better than anywhere else.

But you still haven't answered my question. Why did you pack your bags and leave this country behind you? And don't tell me the usual bullshit. I want to know what it's like seeing this grey river from up above ...

Following the example of Eduardo Mallea (whom I haven't read, in the same way that I haven't read Juan José Saer, who tells the story of the Río de la Plata), I could have told him of the statuesque stillness of the river, of its lack of colour and so on. But, in fact, I don't know what I felt when I saw the Río de la Plata from up there – perhaps nothing, or a desire to forget all about it. And I didn't even know what to tell him about why I left, or how long I'd be away. I just wanted to leave, that was all. There was also the fact that they'd stopped serving me drinks at Tío Pablo's, as they'd done to my cousin – before he left for France he had told me, "I'm off, away from this shithole of a country where there's no money even for a quick shot of *ginebra*. What can I do here, with no money?"

... in April I suddenly found you had left for the Malvinas. It was Irlandés who told me, I remember it well. I was sitting at my

usual table, with half a bottle of Johnnie Walker churning in my stomach. And you know that according to one of the rules at Tío Pablo's, if someone has finished half a bottle of whisky, you're supposed to let him talk and to listen to him, just in case he's got something interesting to say. I stuck to this rule for an hour, but Irlandés kept on repeating, "Can you imagine that jerk down there shooting at the English? I just can't believe it!"

"Listen, Irlandés, do you reckon he'll come back in one piece?" I asked, just to see whether he'd have a go at guessing.

"Of course, he'll dig himself a hole and stay inside 'til we go and bring him back."

And then I plucked up courage and called your family, but even they had nothing to tell me. Your mother started crying on the phone. She said she'd been calling the barracks every day but they couldn't give her any news, they'd let her know as soon as they had some news and so on.

"Don't worry, Señora, he'll be alright, those who go off to war, they don't all get killed!"

You'd got caught up in a fine mess! She also told me about your grandpa. Before ending up in hospital, he had told her not to worry – you'd deal with those English down there perfectly well, he said, in fact they were the ones who ought to be frightened of you; they could have all the weapons in the world, all the helicopters, all the bombs, he said, but those British heads of theirs would always stay exactly the same. I didn't telephone again after that. I realized that your mother became anxious when she talked to me. When I wanted to find out about you, I'd go and wake up Irlandés in the morning – that was the only time of day when he was capable of putting together a few coherent words – and I'd get him to call your mother. She told Irlandés that she wrote you every day, she sat down in front of a saint and filled page after page. Who knows where those letters finished up.

That's why I once wrote to you that nothing on this earth

*can yet stop the imagination and that what seems most
ridiculous is always possible! It is possible that someone like you
could end up in a war getting shot at by the English. Even that!
Thatcher's pirates had been warless for forty years and were
itching for a bit of excitement with somebody ... and you just
happened to be the one who ended up there, in the middle of it,
not even knowing how to hold a gun! They were fighting the first
technological and electronic war in history, while for us it was the
last war of the nineteenth century ...*

I've always kept in touch with Carlitos, if only through these letters
that arrive from Buenos Aires, letters in which he tells me how his
novel is progressing. Sometimes he writes from a small house he
has on an island in the Paraná Delta, where he shuts himself up for
three or four days and is constantly harassed by mosquitoes and by
cockroaches that wander from one hole in the floor to the next.
Every so often the *Dieciocho whisky* magazine or *Bardamu Bardamu*
publishes a story or a short collection of poems, and he always
sends me a copy.

Here's my latest collection of poems, he wrote in one of his recent
letters, *dedicated to the house at Paraná – Entomological ethology and
its therapeutic properties.*

I often get stuck on the first line or two when I try to write back
to him. Carlitos represents that penniless suburban past in which
time, spent drinking beer and reading, seems to have stopped still,
like the surface waters of the Río de la Plata. And these memories
block me at once, and send me back off into the past: *Alberto, please,*
he once wrote, *have you got Proustitus as well? It's getting beyond a
joke. Have you stopped reading Juan Carlos Onetti? Are you still
reading Augusto Roa Bastos?*

Sometimes I want to pick up the phone and call him. And
sometimes I end up saying I'll be back soon, in fact very soon.

"You've been telling me you're coming back for years," Carlitos answers.

"Well, it's true ... I've been wanting to return for years, but I just can't seem to manage it."

Chapter Thirteen

Which tells of my friend Carlitos's future novel and reminds me of a soldier who's unable to run off in the face of the English advance

Buenos Aires

Dear Alberto,

I'm still sitting here at a table at Tío Pablo's, like an upturned tortoise waving its legs in the air. Reality is reality – unfortunately – and when you're forced to draw your legs in, there's nothing that can be done.

Even though you're there in Italy, and you still don't want to talk about the Malvinas, I'm pushing on all the same with my book on the war. And the story I want to tell goes more or less like this: two or three days before the end of the war, a soldier leaves his troop and hides away in an abandoned house close to Puerto Argentino. He stays there waiting for the end of the bombing and towards the end of June he leaves the abandoned house. He walks along the deserted roads until he finds a small warehouse outside the town which the Argentines had used for storing provisions. He doesn't think of himself as a traitor. He takes a few tins of tuna, a few bars of chocolate trodden on the ground, fills his pockets with cigarette ends and other bits and pieces. Outside, on the battlefield, he finds objects that have been left behind: muddy boots, bits of guns, a rainproof poncho, a cooking pot, a helmet, tins of corn, of meat ... There's a lot of wind. He stays in the house until his supply of food runs out. Then he goes back to the warehouse but finds it completely derelict. He carries on walking until he arrives down in the town, where the people pretend not to see him. The kelpers don't want Argentine soldiers around: "We don't want Argentines on our islands," they write on their shop doors. A builder is the only person prepared to look after him. He asks his name, but he tells him he's forgotten it. The builder gives him a windproof jacket to get him through the winter, offers him a job, a place to sleep and a name: Dieguito, like Maradona. The soldier accepts and stays on the islands, working in a building yard. His comrades think he has died in the battle of June 12, two days before the end of the war. The cold, the snow, the Atlantic wind, the deserted roads ... everything begins to become a part of him, as if the islands and the sea had swallowed him up forever. Days go by, one after the other, each the same, passing unnoticed, and he works away in silence. He rubs his hands, shrugs his shoulders. No one knows what matters to him. He lives stroking his beard. Many years later a group of Argentine veterans come on a visit to the islands. Dieguito sees them, they don't recognize him, he's no longer nineteen as he was in 1982, but thirty-eight; he has a long beard and dark blotches on his face. He talks English, though not like a kelper. He follows them in silence, watches their movements, and enjoys hearing someone talking in his mother-tongue. He watches the veterans, now nearing forty themselves, as they clamber over the rocks of Moody Brook, as they go into the old trenches, lift up objects lying there almost buried in the ground, as they go into Darwin Cemetery, look at the names on the crosses and read: "Aquí yace un soldado argentino cuyo nombre sólo conoce Dios," *and hug each other and cry. That is the place where he too lies, the soldier who escaped from the Gurkha offensive and hid in the first abandoned house he could find, with words and a name he no longer wants to remember, because his name by now is Dieguito,* Dieguito el malvinense, *as the old builder calls him.*

The other day, as I was travelling on the General San Martín railway, I saw a war veteran giving out a pamphlet with some photos of the war. He had lost a leg and was asking passengers for a donation. The train was rocking back and forth, and he was moving his crutches to keep his balance. He received no money at all in the carriage where I was travelling. He said nothing. He took all his war pamphlets and went off to try his luck in another carriage. I wanted to tell him I was writing a novel about the Malvinas but then I had second thoughts. I carried on imagining that white and green landscape of the islands which perhaps one day I will go and see, and Dieguito of the Malvinas walking around the edge of a minefield. Three or four strands of barbed wire and every now and then a red sign with a skull in the middle and the words: "Danger mines." He carries on walking and walking, his ears frozen by the cold. From time to time he rests his hands on the fence. Something comes to mind. He attempts a smile. At one point he remembers something funny that happened to him many years before. "Dieguito," says Dieguito. He smiles again. Then he reads the notice and repeats: "Danger mines." He jumps over the fence, looks at the great expanse of mined field and starts walking, just like that, aimlessly, while the penguins scuttle off towards the beach. Someone calls after him from far away: "Dieguito! Dieguito! No, Dieguito, not there!" But he doesn't seem to hear and wanders further in among the mines. "Go back." And he repeats the same words: "Go back, go back." But no one could understand that Dieguito was doing exactly that, he was going back.

I never wrote to tell Carlitos what I thought of the story about Dieguito – I don't suppose he even expected to hear what I thought of it. When I read it the first time, it brought back to mind a soldier I had seen on that very morning of June 12 on Mount Longdon.

The English were attacking us relentlessly. They did it through the night so that we couldn't sleep. Their troops could count on support from the ships that bombarded us from the sea, and from planes that massacred us from the sky, and from well rested soldiers who were continually relieved; whereas we were holed up in trenches, covered in mud and incapable of holding back the offensive. We were forced to fight night and day with no food or sleep. Our sleep was dependent upon the pattern of enemy attacks.

At dawn on June 12, after a night of non-stop bombardment, we felt too exposed to remain any longer in those holes. So they ordered us to pull back immediately towards Puerto Argentina, since the English had never bombed the town; but before pulling back, they told us to destroy the weapons and equipment we were leaving behind on the field so that the enemy couldn't use them in their advance. Our objective from that moment on was to reach the town. The surrender of the Argentine army was imminent. The English gunfire was unremitting. We seemed to hear Gurkha cries everywhere. I failed to understand, however hard I tried, why they were unloading their whole arsenal onto us. I couldn't imagine being any more useless than I was. The air was unbreathable, and I was terrified by those blasts that were thrashing us one after the other. We knew already that it was going to end like this. I wanted to be back under those swarms of parakeets, I thought of my father holding my hand and strolling with me along the riverbank at San Fernando. Death was passing close by, and I wanted to get away, but the world had become so tight around me that I couldn't even move. I had always had the suspicion that the hereafter wasn't so far away and that one day I'd be able to touch it with my hands. But now I was touching the hereafter with body and soul. Two or three Sea Harriers suddenly appeared, flying low. At that moment there was a constant hail of bombs. Some soldiers fled; others carried on replying to the attack (neither the howitzers, which were our largest artillery, nor the anti-aircraft guns could hold back the attack), others were still dreaming up defence tactics; and others were getting blown into the air like rag dolls. I ran and threw myself to the ground, started running again and threw myself down again. At a certain point I got swallowed up by an explosion which spat me out far away. I felt for my legs, my chest, my balls. Everything I should have had was there. The noise of the Sea Harriers was tearing through my ears. I'd liked to have taken any old piece of white rag and waved it with both hands, to put a stop to this pandemonium, to let the British know I was frightened, but I had nothing on me that even resembled a piece of white rag. I had to do something other than running off. I suddenly turned back to our old position and saw the outline of a soldier about thirty metres from me. He was standing, as if paralyzed, covered by a large dark plastic poncho. He was looking up into the sky bewildered, in wonder at what was going on around.

"What the fuck are you doing there, run, run!" I shouted as loudly as my lungs would allow.

I threw myself down once more, put my hands over my ears. A bomb had dropped just a short distance away, lighting up the whole area.

"Run, you idiot!" I kept shouting.

He made no reply. He looked round dazed and confused, turning his head from one side to the other.

"Come! Come here!"

At that point he turned towards me. He opened his arms and then with one hand pointed to the sky. His whole body was sweating. I was still shouting at the top of my voice. I too was paralyzed. I wanted to run towards him, I wanted to run off towards the town ... I'd have done anything not to have been there. At that moment a bomb exploded right by us, and I dived instinctively into the rocks, with my hands over my head. A few seconds later, getting up again, I could see there was nothing now between me and the English advance.

"Where the fuck are you?" I kept shouting. No one answered. All I could hear were the shouts of other soldiers climbing down towards the town, calling out to each other. I never managed to find out who that lad was. They were throwing everything they could at us, with such incredible violence that I couldn't even work out where I was going. I had a fraction of a second to decide. I looked around and started running again; I turned only to check where I was. I was giving everything I could. With each explosion, I pushed my helmet as far down over my head as I could. I didn't want to end up getting killed by a bit of shrapnel stuck who knows where. This whole business was nothing to do with me. I carried on running through the mud for God knows how long. I was stumbling everywhere. I couldn't work out what was going on. I was trying to reach my artillery group, which had scattered in the retreat. I was suddenly swallowed up by an explosion and, a moment later, found myself lying on the ground. I don't know how long I lay like that – a few seconds, an hour. At some point I was aware of someone calling me and slapping me round the face.

"Get up, get up, run… Move yourself!"

I opened my eyes. I was shaking from the cold and couldn't speak. Over me was a dark sky and in the middle the desperate face of a soldier who was saying, "Get up, the Gurkhas are coming. Get up!"

He took me by the hand and put me between a pair of soldiers who were hurrying down; they too were abandoning the hilltop line. We carried on running for hours until we reached a group of soldiers who were walking in silence towards the entrance to the town. I wasn't bleeding, but something had got turned inside my stomach. Every now and then a lone Sea Harrier appeared from the clouds and pointed its wings towards the port, then climbed vertically, before disappearing once again into a chasm among the clouds. I checked I still had Carlitos's book of poems and carried on walking, having reduced my load down to the last bullet. I suddenly remembered one of the poems in *El grito de la langosta*. I looked for it and gave it to a soldier beside me to read it. He stopped, took the book and read one line, or two at most. He then returned the book to me without saying a word, or perhaps he said "Nice." I can't remember. I put the book back in my pocket and carried on walking towards the town.

Chapter Fourteen

About when the English advance reaches the town and how, at the end of the war, the airport becomes our prison camp

Pulling back towards the town, some of us kept our weapons while others arrived with nothing, injured, covered in mud. On the hills, part of the artillery kept fighting and it wasn't clear whether we would surrender straightaway or continue reinforcing the front. But all we could do was wait for the enemy advance, for this disastrous adventure to finish as quickly as possible.

It was ten or fifteen degrees below zero and the sky was dull, lightless. The small town of Puerto Argentino stood between the English advance on one side and the sea on the other, like Purgatory between Heaven and Hell. It was a group of painted houses with sloping roofs, a hospital packed with wounded, a church, a few sheds, the governor's residence where General Menéndez was hiding out, the post office and a series of desolate roads. I had only just arrived in that Purgatory and was now walking its chilly streets with my feet soaked. Every so often I came across a comrade. Each asked for cigarettes or something to eat, but since no one had anything, we each continued on. At a certain point, as I was trying to find shelter from the wind behind the wall of a house, I saw Revueltas with one hand rummaging through a garbage bin, and the other scratching in his trousers. With Revueltas, I already knew there were only two things you could talk about: the tyranny of our military rulers, or how to get rid of crabs.

"Adorno!" he called out, seeing me propped against the wall. "What happened to you?"

"And how about you. Alright?"

"I can't bear them, these stinking crabs."

"You wait, they'll surrender too, when the English arrive."

"Christ Almighty, you see what these military bastards are like? I go to the infirmary and ask for some treatment, and they tell me they have nothing for infections. Jesus, what sort of nurse is it who can't even rid these creatures from my balls?"

Revueltas was a member of my company. He had nothing with him except for a plastic rosary round his neck and the head of a cherub that dangled from his chest. He had dumped everything before entering the town.

"They can keep it, that clapped-out gun," he said.

The soldiers would touch their balls when they saw Revueltas, not because he brought them bad luck but because he had so much bad luck himself. And what was more, he had crabs, and that was a good enough reason for anyone to keep clear of him. In any event, on that day of the retreat, Revueltas's crabs gave me a more practical and human idea of reality.

"So then?" he said, still scratching himself. "Where's Black Pelé?"

"I've no idea. I don't even know how I got here myself. I just remember one soldier. He was standing there. I was shouting, 'Run, run … come here,' but I lost sight of him after that."

Revueltas took a piece of wet bread from the bin where he had been rummaging. I gave him a look of disgust, then he broke it in two and handed me the soggier part. At that moment I thanked him, though I could hardly forget that he'd just been scratching his crab-ridden testicles with one of the hands he was now using to break the bread. We were surrounded by a smell of dust mixed with the smell from things burning on the bonfires along the streets. Some of the soldiers were standing there with their hands stretched out towards the fire, recounting their experiences, while others wandered round collecting things to burn. We had to keep warm and needed to eat. Luckily that night we found some food in a hut by the governor's house and closed ourselves up till the following morning, drinking Velvedere wine, eating raw pasta and several tins of paté. Revueltas kept scratching himself like mad, asking for alcohol, whisky, something to pour on his testicles. He said he'd even be willing to let Lieutenant Owen scratch him. A couple of soldiers from Corrientes arrived at the hut. They had been fighting against the Gurkhas. They said not a word. Just one of them, every now and then, would say, "Poor comrades," then fall silent again. The hours passed, one by one, and there were now only two alternatives: a massacre in the town, or capitulation. Going back to fight would have been difficult. I wasn't the only one who felt like that, nor the only one anxious to become a British prisoner as soon as possible.

"At least they'll give you something to eat and drink," Revueltas said, "and they won't take their frustration out on you, like these sons of bitches."

In the meantime, a couple of soldiers were trying to tune a radio but whenever they found a station the voice of the speaker was drowned by interference. And we couldn't get a clear idea of what was going on.

"Shh! Shut up!" said one of the soldiers. "There's an army bulletin."

The Estado Mayor Conjunto *of the Armed Forces makes the following announcement regarding the military operations of yesterday, 13th June 1982: the Argentine Air Force has made numerous successful strikes against enemy forces with attacks against men and armaments ... The enemy is desperately trying to reorganize its lines of defence, after the substantial losses and casualties so far incurred.*

"Come on ... get an English station and find out what they're saying ... that's enough of these fucking bulletins, always the same bullshit."

A soldier arrived, just back from the military cemetery. He said there were loads of burials going on down there.

"There must have been twenty," he said, "unloaded from a lorry, I saw them. They put them into plastic sacks. Then a bulldozer covered them over, just like that, you understand? Dropping the earth on top of them."

The two from Corrientes got up without saying a word and went off towards the cemetery. I wanted to go too, but for some reason, I don't know why, I stayed there glued to the radio, paralysed. Then Revueltas took a letter out of his helmet which a young girl and her classmates had written. She said she was very proud of us "for defending our sister Malvina… I am twelve, and when I'm eighteen I want to go and see that land and see my flag flying over the Malvinas islands". Revueltas folded the letter up again and put it back in his helmet.

Some soldiers were writing graffiti on the walls with the tip of a knife:

I'm going home.
The Malvinas islands are Argentine
and if they're no longer Argentine
let God sink them. June '82

They appeared, then were gone
I pressed the trigger till my ammo was spent
I must have shot someone.

Luckily the surrender took place the day after, and the British troops entered Puerto Argentino in triumph. General Moore of the British army read the following message in front of the governor's residence: *Today 14th June 1982 at Port Stanley, General Menéndez surrendered in the name of all the Argentine forces. The Falkland*

Islands are once more under the government freely chosen by their inhabitants. God save the Queen.

Finally, we could see the English face to face. White and well fed, with smooth skin and grins on their faces. Often, they didn't look at us, not even when we met, and yet they showed no animosity towards us. By now they were in full control. Jeeps and tanks filed past along the streets. They marched along in twos, wrapped up in their thermal suits. Once they'd reached the town centre, they took down the blue and white flag that had been flying in front of the governor's residence since 2nd April and replaced it with their own. I felt better, even though we'd lost the war. And I had no idea whether that crisscross flag was about to free me from anything. I was used to failure and was quite sure that if I had to live another life, that would be a failure too. Revueltas thought just the same as me.

"Today it's crabs," he said, "tomorrow it will be lectures from your wife, your kidneys the day after ... there'll always be some fucking torment."

The kelpers began to emerge from their homes as soon as the British troops arrived. They jabbered away in English with the new arrivals. Sometimes they insulted us, and we couldn't always understand them: but then they would say, "Fuck you," for example, and we understood that perfectly well. There were others who insulted us not with words but gestures. The islanders felt free again, now the British troops were back. But all this had a strange effect on us. We had been convinced, when we arrived there, that we had come to liberate our own people from British rule.

"Freedom to our people of the Malvinas!" they had shouted before we left.

"And freedom it shall be," we replied.

The war ought to have come smoothly to an end and yet, on the morning of 15th June, Captain Correas assembled all his troops to tell us we had to hand over our guns, helmets and ammunition in the places the English had set up outside the city. And after the handover we had to walk towards the airport.

"The town has to be evacuated. Take your things and get ready to leave," the captain said.

I felt more human without a gun. I was only sorry to be leaving my helmet behind. With nothing on my head, I seemed to have lost some point of reference. Some soldiers kissed their guns before handing them over and let them drop with that pained expression which poor people have when they are parting with their last few coins; others smashed them against the ground so they couldn't be used again. But these gestures certainly didn't worry the English, who would never have dreamt of going off to fight a war with museum pieces like those.

Then we headed off on foot towards the airport. Captain Correas went ahead as we marched. He wanted us to keep our military dignity. Revueltas couldn't stop shuffling and scratching himself. The further we pressed on towards the airport the more desolate the landscape became. Featureless scenery. We were taking the same road we had been on at the start of the war, and now I could only vaguely remember the first day or two from our arrival. I still remembered Lieutenant Owen's orders when he told us to get it clear in our heads that we weren't down there for fun, the English fleet would soon be arriving, we had to stay alert. In the morning, towards the end of April, there was a certain magic on those islands: the southern gulls swooped over the beaches vying for molluscs and crustaceans, others dipped and turned pensively over the breakers, before letting the wind carry them away with hardly a flap of their wings. But now the landscape was different, and we walked silently in single file.

"If we had followed army orders we'd all have been dead by now," Revueltas muttered. I don't know where he found the energy still to come out with such ideas. I think it must have been the crabs that kept his brain active. In any event, he was right, though I didn't manage an answer, and just kept on marching.

"I reckon," I said, my voice barely audible, "these islands would be much nicer if they planted a few trees on them." But Revueltas was too busy scratching himself to listen to conversations like that.

The airport had been the first and last outpost to be defended by the Argentine artillery during those months. From 2nd April it had become the operational centre for every manoeuvre and now, at the end of the war, had been transformed into our prison camp. There were wrecked planes on the runway. Some were burnt out and all that remained were black carcasses which prisoners used to shelter from the cold. Others just had their wings torn off or broken landing gear. On the runway, however, there were large holes filled with water. There were holes also at the sides of the runway, holes everywhere, large, small, whose surface water rippled in the wind. Some of them, I thought, must have been from the thrashing the Sea Harriers had given them during the first bombardment. The hangar and the painted hut beside the runway were miraculously intact. We had no idea how long we would be held at the airport, so we had to look for stuff to build a fire to warm ourselves. I couldn't feel my hands and feet, and when I held something, anything, I didn't have enough force to grip it. Many of the prisoners gathered around a burned-out plane and sang songs by León Gieco or Charly García. There was even someone who had improvised a drum with a piece of sheet metal, and someone else who pretended to dance. Those songs bored me to death and although there was a fire there to warm me, I preferred to go off somewhere else. I wandered around between one group of prisoners and another. I wasn't the only one. Others hid, or placed their arms over their heads, trembling, and stayed like that until someone brought them a cup of *maté cocido*. There was one soldier who went off and got the English to show him their thermal suits.

"They have batteries," he said, "and a little thing to control the temperature." But it was better not to believe certain things.

"Adorno! Come here," Revueltas shouted. He had stopped for a piss and was showing off his parabolic jet from which a dense steam was rising. When I approached, he pulled from his pocket a pair of binoculars he had found, making sure the other soldiers wouldn't see.

"I'm taking them home. What do you reckon?"

"They'll taken them off you before you leave the island."

"I'm not harming anyone if I take a pair of binoculars." They were only binoculars, after all, but some rules were best not broken.

"I don't know. They've told us to leave everything. We're under English command now, remember, and you know what the English are like."

"I haven't a clue what the English are like, and I don't want to know. And if no one tells me to leave them, then I'm taking these binoculars with me."

"Fine, do what you want. But if I were you, I'd leave them to rot here."

Chapter Fifteen

About when Sergeant Alcalde makes us have mock fights with a wooden knife and the day when the barracks' chaplain gives me a hug

During my first days in the army, I rather enjoyed being ordered around like that, wearing broken-down unmatched boots, baggy trousers, having a shaved head, rushing about everywhere; I felt that in this whole world there was one solid, disciplined life, and that a period of austerity under those trees full of parakeets would be good for me. We got up at dawn and, once out of our tents, had to stand to attention, in a line, waiting for roll call; we then went to the latrines in our underpants, running in single file, and it was good to feel the morning chill and hear the parakeets celebrating in the trees above. It was a duty I willingly carried out. The English fleet was about to set sail and the world was filling up with new words: Gurkha, Sea King, Exocet, Mirage, Port Stanley, MB339 and so on. There was a general feeling of excitement during those days: waiting for the war, waiting for the World Cup, the speeches of General Galtieri in Plaza de Mayo, the collecting of funds. It was touching to see how many people reconciled themselves with their oppressors and raised them to the level of great defenders of the nation. "You must consider it an honour to go to the front, fight British imperialism, reclaim the islands they have taken away from us," our military rulers told us.

"Taken away! After 150 years we want to start reclaiming the islands!" said my father, who loathed this patriotic jingoism. "And I tell you what," he added. "If the Malvinas aren't Argentine, this doesn't strike me as such a terrible thing."

And then he started talking about how his house had been seized by the Germans and how, at one point, they started shooting against the allies who were holding the town opposite, and there was constant firing back and forth, and how he watched the bullets whizzing over the roof of his house.

"But now we have the Pucará twin-turbines," I said. "You wait and see ... those Pucarás will send the British anti-aircraft guns mad."

He shook his head, lit a cigarette: "But you reckon you'll manage to look after yourself if they send you down there?"

"You don't think I'm cut out for it, do you?"

My father was quite sure I wasn't, and I didn't have the courage to contradict him.

One day Sergeant Alcalde, who announced he was our battalion's war instructor, brought each of us a wooden knife which we had to use in a mock attack, to overcome our fear of killing.

"The English will try to avoid hand-to-hand combat; everyone knows the Argentine skill with cold weapons. But we need to get them hand-to-hand all the same. They need to understand who they're dealing with. Understood?"

"Understood, sergeant!"

Once he had explained in detail how to use the knife and its advantages, the sergeant, in one of his moments of euphoria, let out the famous *Sapucay* war cry and threw himself like an Indian on the first unfortunate wretch.

"Hell, I want to see some courage! We'll soon be at war, you bunch of fairies," he shouted, "and you'll have to start showing some balls, even if you haven't got any. Our country is behind us, we can't let it down. You understand?"

"Understood, sergeant!" we repeated at the sergeant's incontrovertible order.

"Now put yourselves one against another and start fighting."

News of the war had hardened everyone, from the latest recruit up to the President.

"Didn't they tell us the English have guns with infra-red sights?" I quietly asked one of my comrades.

"No idea, perhaps they'll have a change of mind. Just do what the sergeant says and don't ask questions."

The idea of having to stick a knife into a Gurkha's chest made me almost laugh.

That day, I had to fight with Black Pelé. He managed to floor me in one move every time I attempted to get anywhere near him. I asked him as a favour to let me win at least once, but on certain matters he was inflexible, and he just carried on demonstrating his physical prowess. The sergeant came up soon after and gave me a punch in the chest. As I staggered back, he shouted, "You are an idiot – a faggot who doesn't know how to defend himself! How can we go to war with people like this?"

"Sorry, sergeant. In the war I'll give it all I've got, sergeant!" And although I didn't succeed in getting Black Pelé to the ground, I really was quite certain I wouldn't be the lily-livered faggot the sergeant had called me. I felt sure I'd summon all the courage I'd never shown until then and would amaze all those who had never shown any trust in me, including my father.

Next morning, I asked the sergeant for permission to go to the church in the barracks to say an Our Father and a few Hail Marys. There was a smell of incense, and the sun filtered through a stained-glass window above the altar. I removed my beret, sat in a pew, and after a quarter of an hour stood up, crossed myself in front of the altar and was about to leave when I saw the large profile of the barracks' chaplain in his cassock, standing by the door.

"Good morning, Father."

"Good morning, my son," he replied, putting a hand on my shoulder. And he paused for a while in silence. "These are difficult times for all of us, I know, but we have to remain strong, for it is the will of the Lord."

"But why?" I asked.

"Only God knows that."

He took my hands in his and sat me down in the last pew, beneath the holy-water stoup. Then he asked my name, about my family, and whether I believed in God. Resorting to a pious commonplace, I replied that I believed in a cosmic God.

He then embraced me, moved by the fact that I had gone to church, and I was stuck there in his grip for several seconds. I felt his hands against my back, pulling me ever tighter as though he wanted to prevent my superiors from tearing me from his clutches.

"Thank you, Father, it's very kind of you. I'll always pray," I said.

I tried to disentangle myself, delicately, but he hugged me even more.

"Thank you, Father, thank you," I said again. "I'll do all I can to bring great honour to our country."

When he finally started stroking the back of my head and I felt his stomach in front of me, I wriggled out of his grip, not knowing what to think.

The priest then opened his arms and stared straight at me. He had thick bushy eyebrows, a pink complexion and two vertical creases on either side of his mouth. He ran both hands through his hair and almost whispered, "God is here everywhere and wants us always to remember that. You can be sure he will never fail to answer our prayers."

That evening they assembled us for departure, and by some miracle I managed to say goodbye to my parents at the entrance to the barracks. My mother, my father, my sister, all crying, and as I marched in line towards the airport, I thought maybe Sergeant Alcalde hadn't been entirely wrong in calling me a lily-livered faggot. I was scared, scared as hell. I didn't feel up to my task, I could never pull out a knife or shoot an Englishman – "Sorry, Sergeant, you have to understand." Four or five planes were there in front of us, ready for take-off. From comedy we were gradually sliding into tragedy (no more parakeets, no more the orange dawn on the horizon, no more physical exercises) and the barracks was transformed into a situation of total confusion: "Here's your rucksack! Here's your helmet! Here's your gun and your ammunition! Start showing some balls, even if you haven't any. Long Live Argentina!"

They pushed me into a four-engine plane, and two or three days later I was in the middle of that group of islands in the South Atlantic.

Chapter Sixteen

On the first day of bombing and how two poor sods like me and Huidobro find ourselves on guard while the English are attacking the airport

Various rumours had spread among the soldiers before the war began. Some said it was all just for show, that the English would never bomb us, and the purpose of the war was simply to preserve the power of the military rulers. But others reckoned this would trigger the Third World War because the Russians would step in to defend us, after which the Americans would defend the British, and at that point the Chinese would side with us and the Chileans with them. Then the Peruvians and the Germans would join in, and even the Japanese, who would arm their Pacific Ocean fleet. But the Chileans, who always had it in for the Argentines, would close the Magellan Strait and then there would be bombing to defend the strait, and Tierra del Fuego would then get involved and its name would at last be justified. The whole world, some on one side and some on the other, sending aircraft carriers, destroyers, submarines, fighter squadrons, anti-submarine squadrons, reconnaissance squadrons ... whales, penguins, sea lions, spitting guanacos ...

"That's how world wars begin," they said. "You start by occupying an island, you raise a flag there, the other side says no and so you call someone in to defend you, the other side calls in someone else, and all hell breaks loose."

"I reckon things ought to be sorted out with a football match," said someone else who wanted to have his say.

"Or we could let them win the World Cup, to make them happy."

"Those cretins haven't even qualified."

"That's why they're so pissed off!"

"What are you talking about? England has qualified, of course it has. It's in the same group as France."

"Enough of the bullshit! We're here, and in a few days those bastards are going to massacre us. That's how it is, you've got to be realistic."

"And what do you know about being realistic?"

Realism didn't exist, according to Carlitos. For him it was just an illusion to give a semblance of credibility to something that has never happened. I didn't really understand what he meant at the time, but it seemed an intelligent and pertinent idea. And since at that moment I felt an urge to say something intelligent and pertinent, I added, "You know, I believe that realism in the strict sense doesn't exist, it's all artificial. A game of fantasy. A friend of mine's a poet – he often says that."

"So why don't you ask your friend what the English are coming to do, down here, with all those ships piled up with helicopters? Don't you understand they've got Gurkhas on those fucking ships? Those Nepalese mercenaries will cut your jugular – there's nothing artificial about that."

Fortunately, I was reasonably hopeful, even though events were taking a nasty turn and they were still talking a lot of bullshit about the war – patriotism, sovereignty, and stuff like that. I was tempted more than once to bury my gun in the mud and go to the first officer I could find and say, "That's it, I'm surrendering right now, it's crazy standing here holding a gun – I'm going to the beach, I'll wait down there." They'd have certainly treated me as a traitor or a coward. And yet I had no wish to betray anyone, least of all my comrades. It was a war I just couldn't understand. The idea of waiting for the enemy to arrive, then to start dying in a trench, was something inconceivable. I'd done nothing against the English. "Hold on a bit," I said to myself, "I can die of cirrhosis of the liver, of a broken heart, but I can't be shot by a bullet on a remote island for liberating a few shepherds from British rule. Who knows who these kelpers are, anyway?"

One of the things that happened during that time was the first bombardment of the islands – our first experience of war. The English fleet had left Portsmouth on 5th April and was already nearing the islands. The whole pantomime of war was about to begin. Lieutenant Owen, known to everyone as Billy the Kid because of his quickness with a gun, climbed two or three times a day up a hill near the beach, took off his helmet, laid the butt of his gun on the ground and surveyed the panorama. After that, he would assemble the rest of the company that was meanwhile waiting for him and would tell them what he had worked out. On 30th April, after climbing the hill, he raised his gun and pointed the barrel towards the sea. "The English fleet is at the gates. Between now and tomorrow," he said, still pointing the gun towards the sea, "they will start their air raids. I don't rule out bombardments from the ships, but we have to stop them landing. So keep at the ready, soldiers. God and our country are all that matters now. And we must be true unto death. Ready to give our up lives – our lives – to God and our country."

Someone already knew that the English would start bombarding from the ships the next day, sending out their Sea Kings, but the lieutenant enjoyed playing the prophet.

On 1st May, Fernando Huidobro and I were keeping guard by the sea. A gun round my neck, boots full of mud, a knife in my belt, my helmet on my head, and my hands frozen.

"Always keep your eyes on the sea, never lose sight of it, and report any movement," the lieutenant had told us that day.

"Yes, lieutenant."

"If you see something, raise the alarm straightaway."

"Sure, lieutenant."

"No chattering, always keep alert."

"Understood, lieutenant."

"And make sure you look after your gun. Understood? It's your only companion, remember that, so shove it up your ass if you have to, but never leave it anywhere."

There was a light mist that morning, and it was too cold to sit in the open watching the sea. I found something melancholy about that treeless landscape, with that bitter wind that blew everywhere. Added to which was the expectation of war: waiting for some strange submarine-load of five hundred soldiers suddenly to shoot up the beach and hurl themselves against us. The airport was only a short distance away. It was the vital point the enemy would want to hit right from the start, to knock out all communications with the mainland. I had a plan to save the airport which turned out to be exactly right, though no one ever asked my advice about it. A soldier is never asked what he thinks, he is told just to fight. But the plan I had in my head worked out just right in the end. The point was this. We couldn't match up to British war power. Something therefore had to be done to make sure that the planes could still land. And since the English could only see the condition of the airport from the planes that flew over the area, I thought we could create some sort of scenery that made the pilots think the landing strip had been destroyed. I imagined coloured panels which, seen from high up, would look like craters left by bombs. It would be pointless wasting more bombs, and in this way the airport could still be used right up to the end of the war. When I tried telling this to Lieutenant Owen, he laughed in my face, even though they later used this same tactic and the runway remained more or less intact to the very end.

But if there was one thing I had never imagined, it was that one day I would find myself holding a gun and waiting for a load of bombs to arrive. And now, there I was on guard with Huidobro. There was not a living soul in sight on the promontory where we found ourselves, so I took a sheet of paper from my pocket just for something to do, rested it on my knee and started writing:

My dear Francisca,

In August 1962 some crazy sperm cell in my future father breaks away from the rest of the platoon and goes off on its own sweet way with a cap on its head. Later on, after a few skids, it takes its cap off and goes down some little tubes until it reaches my mother's egg which, at that moment, is in the matrimonial bed. Nine months later, on 30th April 1963, I am born between her legs, wrapped in a placenta. No one ever thought to tell my mother that on the same day, nineteen years later, I would have found myself holding a gun, wearing a helmet, waiting for the English to land.

I refolded the sheet of paper and put it back in my pocket.

"Aren't you scared of being by the sea?" Fernando Huidobro asked, lifting his arm to point out something far away, down in the middle of the water.

"Look, Huidobro, the fact is ... if a plane comes out of the clouds, it won't wait for us to raise the alarm. It'll shoot at us straight away. No time even to say hello, you can be sure of that."

"Don't worry, you can rely on me."

"To do what?"

"To keep a lookout. You carry on writing and taking notes – a record has to be kept of all this."

I wasn't taking notes, I just wanted to go back to the womb and come out when the war was over. There were other soldiers, like Ibañez, who spent their whole time with a pocketbook in their hand, noting down everything. I couldn't take notes about what was happening around me. And while Huidobro was looking out to sea, I took the piece of paper out again and carried on writing to Francisca. I told her that Fernando Huidobro seemed a brave sort who wasn't scared of anything and who, as I was writing, was doing a double lookout, for me and for him.

"Do you reckon they can also shoot us from the ships, if we don't intercept them?" I asked Huidobro, who was still scouring every corner of the area.

"Sure, from ships and aircraft."

"And if on the other hand someone comes down here on foot, what do you do, shoot straightaway?"

"No, first I raise the alarm, then I shoot."

"Have you ever shot anyone?"

"Never, but now I'll shoot quite happily, here, in the chest." Huidobro was convinced about what he was saying and I'm quite sure he would have shot without a second thought because, as he said it, he was stroking the barrel of his gun as you do when you stroke the head of a combat dog.

"I can only do two things, Huidobro – run away and hide or surrender straightaway. To shoot point blank at someone else ... I just can't do it, I swear. Do you see? If someone wants to do something bad to my mother, for example, or to a child, even if I don't know him, and I'm holding a gun, then perhaps I'd close my eyes and fire a couple of shots, just like that, for no reason ... I'm just not capable of shooting for the sake of a few remote islands stuck out there in the Atlantic."

"They're not just any old islands, they're *our* islands and we've got to liberate them."

"Do you feel like someone who's liberating these islands?"

"I feel like someone who's doing his duty."

I realized from the very beginning that the astral conjunction that day was not particularly favourable. Huidobro carried on blindly following Billy the Kid's instructions. He spoke quietly and never took his eyes off the sea.

It was about four in the morning. The day was about to begin, and it wasn't long before the change of guard when we heard a strange sound which, given our circumstances, it was legitimate to regard as hostile. It was a noise that came from the clouds, but then we heard it over our heads. Strong. Threatening. And I don't even know whether at that moment we heard the red alert for the first time, which meant air attack, or just the sound of the two or three planes that appeared from the clouds, heading straight for the airport. If they'd told us those planes had come out of nowhere, like unreal or imaginary beings, we'd have believed them. One of the two, hit maybe by an Argentine anti-aircraft gun, plunged towards the sea, then veered towards us. Huidobro and I ran back yelling and searching for some shelter among the rocks. And as we ran towards the hills, we saw the airport light up with a beautiful orange colour that mushroomed up into the sky; and, in the middle of that god-forsaken world, we discovered for the first time that we really were at war.

"We'll make them pay for it," Huidobro shouted furiously, holding his gun against his chest, as we re-joined the troop. Billy the Kid studied the hangar through his binoculars and cursed. "Fucking English arrogance! Now they'll see who they're dealing with." That day, not just the Royal Air Force but also the Argentine artillery had made their debut.

We heard radio bulletins, one after the other, throughout the day. Luckily, there were no casualties, and the runway was left more or less unscathed, though it was a start that opened up the prospect of a far from promising end.

After the airport bombing, Admiral Woodward of the English fleet demanded the unconditional surrender of the Argentine troops, but the answer from the governor Mario Benjamín Menéndez was clear and determined: "No way. We're the ones who are winning. Send us the young prince instead. Come and get us!" The young prince whom Menéndez was referring to was Prince Andrew, third child of Elizabeth II, who was serving as an officer on the *Invincible*.

How could we know just how rotten was the heroic and idle

soul of a man like Menéndez? In short, Admiral Woodward was demolishing the myth of the insolent Argentine, the myth that *no one can touch me*. And a fantasist like Menéndez couldn't accept the crude reality that Woodward was placing before his very eyes. And that was why our governor became personal: "Send us the young prince and we'll let you see what we're capable of, we Argentines." Unfortunately, there were plenty of others who thought like him. Three days later an English submarine, the *Conqueror*, intercepted the cruiser *Belgrano* on its radar. It sank it with two or three torpedoes. Three hundred and twenty-three Argentine soldiers drowned that day.

"We're the ones who are winning," Menéndez kept saying in the depth of his alcoholic delirium. And Lieutenant Billy the Kid agreed too. "Come here and we'll show you just who we are."

Chapter Seventeen

In which I meet Black Pelé, who is working as a shoe-shiner, and he tells me that Fernando Huidobro is in a psychiatric unit, and in which my dear girlfriend Francisca compels me to stroll past de-Malvinized shop windows

When the sun shone on our front porch, aunt Albertina would go and sit under the lime tree by the flowerbeds. She would wave her fan and keep saying she couldn't wait for the summer to end. She always complained about the flies, even though there was never a single fly in the garden. She sometimes flapped her hands angrily in the air to scare off an imaginary insect or two buzzing around her ears. My mother asked me to keep an eye on her in case she knocked out her hearing aid, which had cost a lot of money. One day I was telling her about when I got off the *Canberra* and returned to the mainland. My aunt meanwhile was peeling an orange with her fingernails and, when I'd finished telling her about my journey as far as Trelew, I realized she had fallen asleep with the half-peeled orange in her hands.

"If you don't want to listen, auntie, I'm going," I told her, getting up from my seat. "I'll see you this evening or tomorrow morning."

And waking up from who knows what dream, she asked, "Have you shut the fridge?"

"Yes, auntie, don't worry." She needed reassuring all the time.

When I reached Francisca's house, I was still thinking about the fridge which perhaps I hadn't shut. I sat in the garden, in the shade, and stayed there gazing at some washing hanging out to dry on a line. Francisca meanwhile was wandering around my seat, and each time she passed close to me she brushed her fingertips against my elbows, then paused and began strolling about again. It was nice to watch her moving around aimlessly. When her mother came out into the garden, she asked why she was hovering around me like an insect.

"Because I like it," Francisca replied. "I like hovering around people like an insect."

For Francisca's mother, there had to be an explanation for every gesture: she was such an irritating woman. Listening to her, it seemed everything had gone wrong in her life, she was never happy. In her eyes, I was some kind of angst-ridden lunatic, like all war veterans, and she scolded her daughter for carrying on with me. "They've got rehabilitation centres, Francisca," she said. "You playing the do-gooder is all we need with all the normal boys there are."

Francisca stopped wandering around me after that and went off to get me a beer. I drank the beer, then suggested we went out. I couldn't have coped with her mother for much longer.

"And where can we go in this heat?"

"While we're thinking you could bring me another beer, if you don't mind." I knew it would take her a while to get it.

In such cases, the best thing was to head towards the train station and decide there. Cicadas in the afternoon heat gave me a sense of boredom. Once we had reached the station we sat down on a bench. We still couldn't decide where to go. In front of us were three shoe-shiners, each with their painted box and all the equipment inside. One man was reading his newspaper with a large black shoe resting on one of the boxes and, once the shoe-shiner had finished his task, he fumbled in his pocket to pay him. The shoe-shiner put the two coins in his pocket and looked across to me. At that same moment I looked at him.

Suddenly I was no longer looking at a shoe-shiner but found myself in front of large green tent with a cross on the entrance flap. A comrade and I are carrying a soldier into the infirmary whose leg has been fractured by the recoil of a gun. There are dead men wrapped in sheets on the beds, and a priest wearing spectacles who is blessing them. A first lieutenant orders us to leave the wounded man on a bed and go straight back to our positions. "Dying is the most natural thing there is, it happens to everyone, but to die fighting means being born again," says the first lieutenant.

At that point, the shoe-shiner got up and approached me.

"Black Pelé, how are you doing?" I asked, in a barely audible voice, though the answer was right there to be seen.

"Here I am, see?" Black Pelé replied. "I'm making a living with these brushes."

It seemed absurd that he, the great barefoot footballer, was there, at the station entrance, cleaning people's shoes. I had seen hardly any of my comrades since the end of the war.

"I saw Espina the other day," said Pelé. "He asked about you. I told him we had met up a couple of times but that I hadn't seen you for months."

"I saw Espina as well, and he asked about you, and I told him more or less the same."

On the brush box was a sticker with a small map of the Malvinas, and across it the Argentine flag and the words "*Las Malvinas son nuestras.*"

"You've heard about Fernando Huidobro?" Pelé asked, after we'd been standing there for a while saying nothing.

"No, what's he done?"

"He's in a psychiatric unit. They say he's scared of everything, poor Huidobro. He hides under the bed as soon as he sees someone."

"I knew he was ill, but I didn't think ..."

"And you knew about Ramón Almeida?"

"Ramón Almeida! The one who boasted he'd never had a bath, remember?"

"That's right"

"What's he done?"

"Didn't Espina tell you?"

"No, he said nothing."

"He didn't make it … he left home … jumped to his death."

"But what are you saying?"

"That's what I've heard. And Ginger Salinas, you've heard about him?"

"Don't tell me Ginger Salinas has killed himself as well?"

"He swallowed a bottle of sleeping tablets."

"Hell! When?"

"A couple of months ago, I think. You remember when he left the trench to go for a crap, because Saucedo didn't want him to crap in the trench? He went behind a rock and two minutes later a bomb dropped and blew up Saucedo, the trench and everything inside it. Remember? Ginger Salinas had been saved by his bowels."

"Christ, and not even that could save him now. Listen, what about going for a beer?" I asked.

Francisca, meanwhile, went to get two tickets and we had a couple of beers at the station bar. I didn't know what to say, or rather what to think. That afternoon I wanted to get back home and shut myself in my room.

"You remember that goose? Fucking hell, you were a good shot, with those clapped-out guns," I said, just for something to say.

"What do you reckon on doing, Alberto? Why don't you come to the meetings? Two or three times a week, we're all there, more or less. We have a chat, tell a few stories. People need to know we're here."

"I don't know. I can't manage anything. I get up in the morning and then I can't wait to get back to bed."

Before saying goodbye, we agreed that one day I'd go and take him to see Huidobro.

"I'll be waiting for you," said Pelé, taking off his beret.

We shook hands and then I went off to join Francisca, who was waiting for me on the bench.

"I've got tickets for Retiro," she said. "We can go to Plaza San Martín and then go up Florida Street and look at the shop windows."

"Shop windows? But what's got into you? Shop windows!"

"What's wrong?"

"Nothing."

"So let's go. I need a pair of slacks."

After seeing Black Pelé shining people's shoes, perhaps she couldn't understand that shop windows just made me feel sick. And although she might think it poetic or even romantic for someone back from a war against the English to set himself up cleaning shoes because no one would give him a proper job, I just couldn't get him out of my mind.

"Listen, Francisca, I can't go window shopping. I'd go with you willingly but my grandpa's dead, my aunt Albertina's going off her head, Black Pelé's working as a shoe-shiner and poor Huidobro's hiding himself under his bed. I'm just a bit confused."

Francisca held her finger up against her lips and then kissed me with an innocence that was half real and half fake. "Don't start that, please. We are now going to Plaza San Martín and then we're going up Florida Street so that I can look for a pair of slacks. You'll be fine, you see. Otherwise, we can have a mint tea, and I'll pay."

"But you don't know what Black Pelé told me. You can't understand…"

"Listen, Alberto, stop this complaining. You should be thankful you came back in one piece."

"One piece? What do you mean, one piece?"

We got onto the train. Francisca was still talking about her slacks, while I was thinking that everything was going on as if there were two levels: one in which things happen and change, the level of life, always now; the other in which things remain as if suspended, the level of expectation, of memories. And when this level entered the first level, I would get stabbing pains at the back of my head. And when I didn't get the stabbing pains at the back of my head, I'd go for a beer at Tío Pablo's. In that way I'd go Malvinizing, thinking about Fiorito, Cardena, Zukovskij the Little Russian, thinking also about that jerk Sergeant Alcalde and all those who thought they were heroes because they wore a uniform. I've never been one of those who want to change the world. Without Sergeant Alcalde, for example, the world for me would have no reason to exist, even though he often enjoyed humiliating us in front of the others, with that cirrhotic face of his. He behaved in that ruthless manner out of need, otherwise his world would have collapsed right around him. We were his support. I therefore knew he had to do what he did, he had no choice; but on the other hand, he was weak, and weakness was viewed with contempt in the military world, and so he had to make himself believable: he had to play at being someone he couldn't be; and for me that was fine, by which I mean I understood it, even though I found it amazing, even incomprehensible, that the biggest shits always managed to get out alive. And so it was fine by me that the world marched on, dragging those who were dead behind it. All of us have to die sooner or later, I said to myself. But how could I walk along Florida Street shopping? How could I cope with the idea that my girlfriend didn't understand that a part of me was still there crouching down under the roof of a timeless trench, waiting for artillery to flatten the side of the mountain?

About an hour later we were under the shade of the great *ombú* tree in Plaza San Martín. We exchanged a few kisses and a caress. Francisca closed her eyes and smiled. Then we started walking along Florida Street, and immediately the procession began along the de-Malvinized shop windows, during which I tried in silence to forget all about meeting my friend Pelé.

Chapter Eighteen

About the day when Black Pelé and I go to visit Huidobro at the psychiatric unit and as soon as we leave we cling onto two bottles of beer

We called him Huidobro, even though his first name was Fernando, Fernando Huidobro – that was what he answered to on the roll call when he came out of the tent half asleep, wearing his baggy underpants and sleeveless string vest.

"Present!" said Huidobro.

"Present, what?"

"Present, sergeant!" he shouted as loud as he could.

"Present, sergeant," Sergeant Alcalde repeated between his teeth. "Wake up then, once and for all."

As time went on, he became just Huidobro. But in the psychiatric unit he was called *Fernandito*: the nurses called him *Fernandito mío*, the doctors called him *Fernando Huidobro* and the dwarf who sat at the clinic entrance with a bit of paper asking everyone the reason for their visit called him *the screwball from the war*.

"We're his friends from the army," Black Pelé and I said, when we went to see him.

"But that screwball never talks," said the dwarf as he was taking us down the corridor.

"Perhaps there's a reason, no?"

"Someone said the English had cut his tongue out," ventured the dwarf.

Along the clinic corridor there were people moving constantly back and forth; others were sitting on benches calling someone's name. There was an air of routine about everything in there.

"This is the room," the dwarf told us as soon as we arrived at Huidobro's door. The nurse, who was at the foot of the bed at that moment, turned to Huidobro, stroked his arm and said, "Fernandito, look! Your friends have come to see you."

But Fernandito remained sitting on the side of the bed, staring at the white wall in front of him. And as he stared at the discoloured whiteness, I saw him once again holding his gun, trudging cold through the mud.

"Come on, Fernandito," the nurse continued. "We'll take a walk later in the courtyard; would you like that? Now stay with your friends, I'll be back in a while."

Huidobro remained sitting there on the edge of his bed with one shoulder twisted to one side and his eyes fixed straight ahead. It was the first time I'd seen him with long hair sticking straight up. The only straight things in that room were his hair and a light which hung down from the ceiling.

"How are you?" Pelé asked, moving as close as he could to him. "We've come to visit you, see?" But Huidobro just carried on looking at the wall, saying nothing.

At that moment, among the many things whirling around in my head, I remembered the time when Monkey Medina (a soldier who'd had the luck, thanks to a good word from his uncle, to land at Puerto Argentino on 2nd April and then to return straight to barracks) had told us he'd been to visit Huidobro. "I saw Huidobro!" said Medina in amazement. "He looks like a Mapuche mask, one of those masks that you can't work out what they're supposed to be." And now that I saw him with his eyes fixed at the wall, I repeated to myself Medina's words even though, to be honest, I've never seen a Mapuche mask and don't even know if the Mapuche people make masks; but to think that Huidobro looked like a Mapuche mask was something that gave him a certain dignity. "When I saw him the first time," Medina said, "he hid under the bed

122

and stayed there the whole time, huddled up, not saying a word. I said to him, 'But what are you doing, Huidobro, don't you remember? It's me, Monkey Medina.' But Huidobro was holding on to the leg of the bed, frightened I was going to drag him out. Then I had the unfortunate idea of bending down under the bed to talk to him close up, like this, eye to eye; at which point Huidobro started yelling at the top of his voice and carried on doing so until two nurses came in and asked me to leave. And as we were talking outside the room, I saw Huidobro get up and go back to bed again." That was what Medina told me about when he'd gone to visit him.

The nurses left us alone and closed the door, which looked out onto a narrow and noisy corridor. I glanced at Black Pelé and Black Pelé glanced at me. I thought about how many things Huidobro could no longer tell us and how many of his family knew nothing about what had happened to him.

"Let's try standing in front of the wall, let's see if he asks us to move," I said.

"You try, seeing that you're so full of ideas," said Pelé.

Huidobro then turned his eyes towards us as though he were looking for some point of reference. In some way it reminded me of how Irlandés used to look, late at night.

"Hi, Huidobro," said Black Pelé, "how are you doing?" but Huidobro just carried on looking at us in absolute silence.

"Good to see you again. We've been wanting to come and visit you for a long while, you know?" Pelé continued.

Huidobro moved his shoulders, as if he wanted to get rid of something that was weighing down on him, then suddenly he stood up with his hands to his sides, like when in the barracks we saw a superior go past and we had to stand to attention. And he stayed like that, with his head slightly crooked, for a minute or so.

"Yes colonel ... yes, sir!" he said loudly, in that tone of voice typical of the barracks; then he turned once more towards the wall and went back to staring at it in silence, as before.

Pelé went a little closer to Huidobro's bed and then, turning to me, asked me whether I thought his soul was in the right place.

"In what sense?"

"In the sense that I reckon sometimes there's something which at a certain point moves it, and it puts it out of line."

"I've no idea, it's difficult to tell."

Black Pelé, the great footballer, always thought things out in anatomical terms.

When the nurses came back, they found Huidobro exactly as they had left him: sitting on the bed, his hair sticking up and his eyes expressionless.

"So, Fernandito, what have your friends been telling you? Aren't you pleased they've come to see you?" asked one of the nurses, a woman who seemed to move with difficulty around the narrow corridors. "A step at a time, Fernandito, okay?" she said, still stroking his cheeks. "You see, little by little you'll get better."

On the bedside cupboard was a photograph of Huidobro at fifteen with long hair, and a girl beside him with dark hair and the kind of fringe that was much in fashion then. They were both in short trousers and smiling at the camera.

Huidobro gave no reply to the nurse, as was predictable. We said goodbye, left the room behind us and, following a narrow corridor that led past a small ward with closed doors, arrived at the hospital yard. That was when Black Pelé told me he was quite happy scraping a living as a shoe shiner. After the Malvinas, he said, it was something he could manage without difficulty. I thought much the same thing. I couldn't have done anything other than what I was doing, in other words, getting up in the morning, going to the library to read Plotinus, and closing myself up in the evening at Tío Pablo's.

Once out of the hospital we sat down at a bar and clung like desperate men onto two bottles of beer. Then another two. And we carried on drinking until we had recovered from the shock and more or less come to terms with the situation. Pelé still insisted that Huidobro's soul had got out of place, like a twisted ankle.

Later, I went with him to collect his box and brushes. He needed to get back to the station, he said, since there were plenty of people returning from the city centre at that hour wanting a shoeshine before they returned home. And I, who at that moment couldn't cope with being alone, went home to get Plotinus's *Enneads* and headed off to the library. This was the only book, I thought, that might help me sort myself out. Each time I read the *Enneads* I thought of my friend Juan Porfirio. Some time ago he had been to Patagonia to search for his wife, who had run away from home, taking their two-and-a-half-year-old child with her. He'd written me a letter from El Bolsón to say he'd found her at last; he had bought an old caravan and set it up close to some woods. He was happy he could see his daughter each day. In the postscript he suggested I should read the life of Plotinus, written by his namesake Porphyry, *who had composed it,* Juan said, *at the age of sixty-eight, after becoming acquainted and united to the great truth. As you see, we Porphyrys always concern ourselves with the life of others ... we construct our own lives over that of others.* Juan's letter had touched me so much that, as well as reading the life of Plotinus as he recommended, I had also started on the *Enneads*, which Porphyry himself had rearranged and published. And that day, after leaving Black Pelé, I remained in the library until the librarian said, "So, my lad, do you aspire to the immaterial, like Plotinus?"

"No," I said.

"So why are you reading him?"

"I don't know, perhaps out of solidarity for a friend of mine ... I'm quite sure he aspires to immateriality."

I closed my book, headed off to Tío Pablo's, and sat there thinking that if I aspired to immateriality too, then some things might have worked out better.

Chapter Nineteen

Which tells of an evening when I'm going to Francisca's house and am followed by a dog which guides me through the night and how Francisca's father, an overgrown boy scout, calls me a moron

A month after my visit to Huidobro, I found myself thinking once more about those voices and the barrage of fists banging on the doors along the hospital corridors, and I wondered whether I could ever go back to being that boy who smoked joints from morning to evening and had the whole world in his grasp. Perhaps all I needed was a hug, a few loving words and a chance of freeing myself from the ghosts that tortured me at night – what they call having your feet on the ground. But I didn't have any of this, so one night, sitting at a table at Tío Pablo's with Irlandés, I came to the dramatic conclusion that I would never manage to sort myself out in this city which was becoming more and more de-Malvinized. Everything was going round the wrong way that evening, and what was more, Irlandés was there talking about the poetry of Carlitos and looking at me with his squint eyes. All Irlandés' talk about Carlitonian poetics, all his pomposity, spurred me there and then to down my beer in one gulp and go off to Francisca's house to tell her about when I was in the trenches and felt the blasts of the bombs which the English were throwing at us and when I fainted because my stomach had shrunk to nothing ... and that in those moments of fear I thought only of her and all the beautiful things we used to say to each other. I moved the chair back, told the barman to put the beers on my account, then wandered off along the dark streets of the district. After four blocks, a dog came up and started walking along with me. It was very hot, and it didn't bark like some of those dogs who spend their day behind a fence. I couldn't hear even the sound of its paws on the pavement. It looked at me silently, and that was all. Perhaps it thought I too was a night animal that roamed the district in the same way. Then it started circling me and brushing against my legs, except when someone opened a window or looked down from a balcony. Then it would stop, let me walk on a few paces, prick up its ears, and give out a bark of the strangest kind that was nothing like the way dogs bark in the daytime. When I finally arrived at Francisca's house, the dog paused by the front door, as if it already knew that was where I was going, then looked me straight in the eye. I tried to give a smile of reassurance.

"Don't worry. It'll all be okay. Let me ring the doorbell, then you can leave me alone."

The dog moved to one side to let me pass, and then went off, not looking back. It paused to drink some water from a puddle, then disappeared silently into the darkness. I rang the doorbell and soon after I heard the voice of Francisca's father.

"Who is it?" he asked over the intercom, but as I said nothing, since his tone of voice didn't seem altogether welcoming, he asked again, "Who is it?" more insistent than before, convinced I hadn't heard. I remembered at that moment how, a few days before my departure, he had told me he'd been boy scout since he was a boy. He said he knew the names of all the trees and all the stars, that he could even recognize the song of a chaffinch or a thrush in the middle of a wood.

"Who is it?" he asked for the third time, even louder.

I took a deep breath before answering and then, hiding myself behind a thin castrato voice, I said, "It's me."

"Me, who?"

"Me, Alberto. I'm looking for Francisca."

"Alberto? You know that respectable folk are usually sleeping at this hour and don't go knocking other people's doors? Francisca's asleep."

"I wanted to tell her something important."

"Important? It's got to be something important, very important."

"Extremely important."

He let out a huff and then, turning to his wife, I could hear him say, "It's that moron! He says he's got something important to say to Francisca."

"What is it?" asked the mother.

"How do I know? He's come soft in the head, that one."

I pictured him at that moment dressed as a boy scout, with short trousers and hairy legs, flicking tufts of grass with a stick.

"Francisca!" her mother shouted from her bedroom. "You're wanted. See what it is, then go straight back to bed."

After a few minutes the door lurched opened and Francisca appeared, wrapped in a white dressing gown with blue and yellow flowers on it. From the first time we knew each other, life had made every attempt to separate us, and since it had so far failed, it had sent me off instead to war, and forced her into chastity. And yet, despite everything, I was still there and now found myself in front of that puzzled, sleepy gaze.

"Have you come from Tío Pablo's?" she asked without even a smile.

"What's Tío Pablo's got to do with it? I've come to see you."

"To see me? You could find another time to come and see me."

"Well, I've found it now. I've come to tell you I want to be with you. I thought, perhaps, we could start to break this abstinence. Even now, straight away. I've been back here quite some while. You know, there were Gurkhas down there, and the rest of it. But I found time all the same to write to you. I told you everything in my letters, remember? Even your mother was happy: 'Here's our hero who's leaving for the Malvinas to defend the flag,' she said. And your father too: 'Our hero, our hero.' I never wanted to be a hero, but nor do I want to drown my liver with alcohol. All I want is a hug, a word to cling to, that's all. Who cares if your folks say I've come back half-stupid?"

She looked at me without saying a word, her arms crossed, brushing the occasional strand of hair from her face.

"That's what I came here for. Can't you see what you're taking away from me?"

My reply came from the voice of her mother that arrived clearly from upstairs. "Francisca! It's no time to be talking outside. Go back to bed and shut the door."

Even that night dog knew that if we'd been successful in ridding those islands of the English her mother would have let her talk to me all night.

"Francisca, I said come back to bed and close the door. If your friend can't sleep then let him go and pester someone else."

Francisca was still looking at me, not saying a word, and then she closed the door. That was it! I was back in the middle of the street. I whistled a couple of times to see whether the dog would come back, but it too had disappeared into the night. I set off home in silence, walking through the cones of lamplight along the streets. Then I thought about Plotinus's *Enneads*, about things that aspire to the complete and perfect unity of God, about the unreality of life and all those fine things that are no use at all when someone shuts the door in your face.